# CRESCENT CITY MURDER

## ALEC PECHE

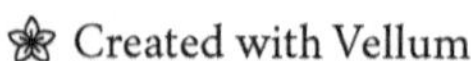 Created with Vellum

# ACKNOWLEDGMENTS

**Acknowledgements**...Many thanks to my first reader and my editor for improving the quality of the story and my writing! Also, deepest gratitude to the medical examiner of New Orleans for granting me a tour of the facility and description of her work.

Alec Peche

# THE HORN..

*The mist is risen like thin breath;*
*The young leaves of the ground smell chill,*
*So faintly are they strewn on death,*
*The road I came down a west hill;*
*But none can name as I can name*
*A little golden-bright thing flame,*
*Since bones have caught their marrow chill.*

*Excerpt from "The Horn" by Léonie Adams*

# CHAPTER 1

$\mathcal{J}$ulien Cheval drove along a quiet road having left the interstate a few miles ago. He slowed looking at a field of soybeans. The leaves were brown on the edge, yet the soil looked moist. He studied the field and judged it was in the early stages of dying. His guess was the drift of a weed killer called Dicamba had damaged the field. The Louisiana Agricultural division had its supervisors on the lookout for such problems as lawsuits and sometimes even fist-fights developed between farmers. The weed killer's manufacturer had issued alerts about using the product, but still crops were damaged. He parked his truck, and walked back to its compartments to get his collection materials. He could hear the hum of insects and not much more in this vast array of farm acreage. Five minutes later he stood up, his collection bags sealed, preparing to move on to the next farm.

As he straightened, he noticed a cloud of dust in the distance. Following the line of dust it appeared that a vehicle was coming toward him from a field access dirt road. He squinted trying to determine if the road belonged to the farm he was standing before or was it a neighbor's? He watched the approach of dust, still not clearly seeing the source of it as he placed his collection envelopes in the slot on the compartment. He finished and walked to the driver's side planning on leaving the area, when the source of dust popped up on the road in front of his truck. He stood there leaning against the driver side door waiting for the dust cloud to disperse. Waving at the dust heading his way in an effort to clear his vision, he finally saw the source.

A large black pick-up truck with wheels more suited to a Saturday night monster truck jam appeared before his clearing vision. The grill on the front gave the impression that it was ready to eat him and his utility truck as a snack. Then he noticed two men in the back of the truck bed. They had the look of ex-military commandos in their dress, posture, and glare. They were seated behind rifles mounted in the truck bed like this field belonged in a war zone.

'What the fuck?' Thought Julien. When had collecting plant samples become so dangerous?

He stood there leaning against his truck door waiting for them to say something. He could feel sweat trickling down his back both from the humidity and his response to the appearance of the truck and its occupants. He could feel his heart racing and his breath accelerate. He saw one of the men in the truck bed pull something off his utility belt. Julien was worried that it was a gun and his thoughts drifted to his son that morning. Had he told him he loved him?

The man brought something up in his hands and Julien's pounding heart momentarily squeezed feeling the impact of a bullet slamming into his chest as he closed his eyes. A few minutes later, when he heard no sound other than the click of the truck's engine he opened his eyes and stared as the commando raised a camera and took a picture of Julien's face.

Julien wondered what kind of idiotic look he'd had on his face for the picture, given the shock and awe of the situation he'd found himself in. He was about to call out a question as to who they were and what they were doing when with a murmured word he couldn't hear, the monster truck spun around and made its dusty way back to whence it came. He let out a breath he didn't realize he'd been holding only to break into a paroxysmal of coughing as the new dust cloud entered his lungs and eyes. As soon as his vision cleared for the second time, he decided it was time to get the hell out of this area and return to more civilized surroundings. Ten minutes later, he was back on the interstate heading for his office building in the Louisiana capital. After the shaky experience that morning, he planned to stay in the office for the remainder of the day. He had plenty of paperwork to catch up on, and after the experience with the truck, he'd inhaled enough dust. If he ran into his supervisor, John, he'd tell him about the strange encounter.

As he pulled into the parking lot of his office, he glanced around him at the traffic moving smoothly down the street in Baton Rouge. The episode with the truck had felt surreal, more so now that he was smack in the middle of civilization so he shrugged and walked into the two-story concrete building carrying his samples from the fields he visited that day.

An hour later, he had his samples processed, paperwork completed, and envelopes to the testing lab in the out-box of his department. Julien connected with a friend from another division, and they walked down the street for lunch. Again as they walked, he thought about telling the friend of his strange incident with the truck and decided to see what he said.

"Hey Keith, I had a weird experience this morning and I wondered if it had ever happened to you?"

With a laugh, Keith replied, "I've had all kinds of weird experiences out in the fields. What happened?"

Julien described his interaction with the monster truck. Keith agreed it was weird, but he hadn't had any interactions with any large trucks, even though he saw any number of similar farms north and west of Baton Rouge.

"Have you seen farms affected by Dicamba – wilted leaves on the way to the plants dying?"

Keith nodded in response, "Not often, maybe once a month."

"Hmmm, well this field I'd stopped at had the classic signs of Dicamba damage. I was tempted to take a sample of the healthy field next to it, but I was distracted by the appearance of the truck."

"I admit I'd probably be shaken if I was alone with a monster truck filled with two men sitting behind rifles. I'll keep an eye out going forward and let you know if I have any strange encounters."

With that, the two men moved their conversation to football and their beloved local teams – the Saints and the LSU Tigers. Julien soon forgot his encounter of the morning once the two men were deep in discussion about LSU hitting a new low in the football world with a loss to Troy.

The remainder of the week proved uneventful for Julien other than he felt like he was coming down with the flu, experiencing nausea after returning from collecting samples out in the field. He guessed that his luck was ending with never having the flu this year, or perhaps the vaccine wasn't as effective this flu season as he'd had his flu shot a few weeks ago.

Julien felt better by the end of the weekend and had enjoyed teaching his son how to play T-ball. The flu receded and he was ready to tackle his role as a state agriculture inspector on Monday. His interaction with the truck and the samples he'd collected ended up filed in the deep recesses of his brain as he moved on to the current issues of his work and private life.

The nausea continued off and on for the next couple of weeks and Julien assumed at first it was the lingering effects of that initial case of flu. Then he began to wonder if he'd been exposed to Dicamba in all the dust that monster truck had stirred up. He checked out the symptoms on the internet, and they matched what he was feeling except for the burning lungs, but he hadn't begun to feel really bad until about two weeks after his exposure to the farm dust of the truck, so that didn't make sense.

It was getting hard to eat because of the nausea and he'd lost weight. He made an appointment to see his doctor and he'd begun to worry he might have something serious like stomach cancer which made him fret more. He felt a little better after he had lunch and then he returned to the field for the collection of more samples. It was a hot and humid day, and he thanked the state for affixing the water jug on the back of their state vehicles. If they hadn't, then Julien would have had to carry water himself. By the end of the day he was getting hit with another wave of nausea so bad that he found himself vomiting in the last field. He returned to his office, pale and tired, wrote a note to follow up on the samples from the field and went home.

"Julien love, what's wrong?" asked his mom when he entered the house he shared with her and his son. Julien was thirty-three years old, thin, worried. His face had a haunted look to it with bloodshot eyes and deep dark circles under his eyes against his ebony skin.

"I don't feel good. The nausea is so bad that I had to vomit before I came home. I'm just going to go lie down in my room. Thank god Jayden is with his mother, I wouldn't make a very good father right now," he said as he turned away and headed toward his bedroom.

"Do you want me to take you to the doctor?"

"I've been to my doctor and he couldn't figure out what was causing my problem. I have an appointment next week with the stomach specialist so all I can do is wait."

"Maybe you should take some time off work to stay home and heal."

"I can't. I don't have much time on the books since I took time off three months ago for Jayden's appendectomy."

His mother frowned and looked on with concern as he walked up the stairs toward his bedroom, hand on his belly. She worried as he didn't look good and he'd lost weight. He had the appointment next week and perhaps that was all they could do – wait to see the specialist. She went into her kitchen and thought about what she might fix for him that would settle his stomach.

She worked on making him Cajun ginger chicken soup and some ginger cookies. That would nourish him and the ginger would settle his stomach.

# CHAPTER 2

The following week, Julien's health only got worse, he was continuing to drop weight and hallucinations began to occur. His mother was beside herself with worry. The visit to the specialist resulted in tests and medication being prescribed. Again he saw improvement over the weekend and so they both thought the new drug was working. Monday dawned hot and humid, and Julien had lots of work to catch up on in the field. He was feeling better this Monday than the previous week so it was time to get in his utility truck and collect more samples.

He made a note and left it on his desk to follow up on the sample from a couple of weeks ago when he'd had that interaction with the monster truck once he returned from the field that afternoon. He didn't want to lose time powering up his computer to check now, besides he'd have time later when he returned to the office.

The day started out great, but by lunch hour, the nausea had returned as bad as ever. He decided to return to the office and not go out in the field anymore that day and this whole week if he could get away with it. His supervisor might notice him being in the office a little too much, but the alternative was calling in sick to work. When he returned, he saw the note reminding him to look up the monster truck field sample as he liked to call it. He logged in and began searching for the results. The computer said the sample was still being processed.

"That's strange," he said out loud.

"What's strange?" asked Kevin making Julien jump as he had no idea that he was close by and working in his cubicle.

"Remember that experience with the monster truck I told you a few weeks ago?"

"Yeah, did you have another meeting?"

"No, but the sample I collected is listed by the computer as still processing. It never takes that long. I should have a result by now."

"Remind me what you took a sample of?

"Dicamba contamination in a crop."

"Hmmm, you're right it should have been posted by now. I get those tests back usually in a week."

"I'll call the lab and see what's happening," Julien said.

Julien retrieved the paperwork on the specimen and looked up the number for the lab. Five minutes later he hung up the phone and called out to Kevin.

"Boy did I get the runaround on that one. First, they told me it was still being processed, then they said it was delayed because the analyzer that processes that specimen was down for repairs which I challenged since I've gotten other results back after this specimen, then finally the lab asked me to get another specimen as they lost my first one."

"That's odd; they've never lost a specimen of mine."

"This is a first for me as well. Oh well, there's nothing I can do today as I wasn't planning on going back out into the field. I'm a little nauseous."

"You want me to collect it for you?"

"Honestly, I've been wondering if my nausea is due to exposure to Dicamba in that field. It started the next day after I took that sample. I wouldn't want to expose you to the misery I've been suffering from. I'll collect it on the way to work tomorrow and resubmit it to the lab."

Julien continued to work from the office for the remainder of the day even though his nausea was distracting to his work. He took his utility truck home rather than his personal vehicle as it contained the equipment he needed to process another sample. He spent the one hour drive home thinking about his symptoms and wondering if it was Dicamba or was someone poisoning him.

If he was being poisoned he needed to align the onset of symptoms with the food he ate and the water he drank. He thought about the water jug on the back of his truck. Maybe someone had put something in that. Tonight when he got home he would wash it out with bleach before using it the next day. He could bring his own water, but the bottles didn't stay cool like the water in the jug did and besides once he bleached it out, whatever bacterial or contaminate that was causing his nausea would be gone, and the jug would be safe again. He did as planned and his mother watched with worried eyes as she listened to his story of the nausea rebounding.

"Julien love, have you thought about quitting that job if it's making you sick?"

"No mama. I've worked there over ten years and I've got good insurance and I had a job immediately after Hurricane Katrina unlike so many of our neighbors. I'm vested in the retirement plan and I like my work. It's rewarding to help farmers with their crops."

"Yeah baby, but it's making you sick. You were never thick to start with and now I would guess you've lost ten pounds in the past month. I'm really concerned. You had a good weekend and then you went back to work and immediately felt bad. Maybe it's the building you work in."

"No mama, I'm not going to quit and I was out in the field when the nausea hit today so it's not the office. I was drinking a lot of water from the jug because it was so hot and that's what made me think that there was some contaminates in the water jug. Now that I've cleaned it a few times with bleach, I'll be fine. I'm going to go lay down now. I'm worn out with nausea and then standing over the jug while washing it with bleach didn't do me any favors."

Mrs. Cheval looked with deep worry at her son's retreating back. He looked ill. She looked over at the jug and decided to bleach it out again just for good measure and went to work.

The next day Julien was only slightly nauseous as he drove to the monster truck field on the way to work. He wanted to grab a sample as quickly as possible to avoid another interaction with the monster truck. He would stop and snip two samples and throw them in two already labeled specimen bags, and then he would leave the field. He anticipated sixty seconds max which would allow him to avoid any dust cloud caused by the monster truck wheels. His survey method went as planned and as he drove away from the field he looked in his rearview mirror and saw an ominous dust cloud behind him. He continued to watch it, but he didn't see the truck as he hit the freeway on-ramp on his way to the office. He smiled, feeling confident that good times were in front of him. He'd collected that sample, the truck hadn't caught him and he had a clean water jug on the back of his truck, so no more nausea. His day went as planned and he was in a cheerful mood when he picked up his son after work.

He had a great evening with his mom and son and had a great appetite. He helped the boy with his homework and got a snack from the kitchen thinking maybe he could put some weight back on now. After a good night's sleep, he dropped his son off at school and returned to work determined to get back out in the field. It was his last good day on earth.

When he returned to the field the next day, it was another hot and humid day and he drank water all morning feeling confident to do so with his clean jug. He soon found himself nauseated when he returned to the office. On his way home that night his driving was erratic and it was only a lack of cars to hit that likely kept him safe on the road. He texted a co-worker to see if he could hitch a ride with him the next day and when he reached home he vowed to never again drink water from the jug on the back of his truck. After a brief conversation with his mother, he declined dinner, and went to his room. Throughout the evening he saw people and animals in the shadows of his bedroom.

His mother stopped in his room when she heard him talking, "Julien love, would you like some of that Ginger soup to settle your stomach?"

He declined and said, "Mama, I'm not feeling well and grandpa is talking to me in the corner," pointing to the empty corner of the room.

"Oh baby, grandpa died in the hurricane, there's nobody in the corner," with fear in her voice. "Do you need to go to the hospital? You're seeing things that aren't there, you're not eating, and you're feeling terrible."

"No mama, I'll feel better in the morning, I just need to rest. I've got a co-worker driving me to work tomorrow."

"That's good Julien, but you should stay home."

"Go away mama, love you."

Mrs. Cheval closed the door and leaned against the wall. What should she do? He was a grown man so she couldn't force him to do anything. She checked on him through the night but she couldn't see a need to call an ambulance and force him to the hospital.

Julien got ready to leave the next morning and found a bottle of ginger ale sitting on the counter for him with a note from mama. He took it as he exited the door to meet his coworker. He still felt terrible and he opened the bottle and took some sips of the soda. Even that didn't help and he had to ask his friend to pull over so he could heave. He told his friend to continue into the office and he'd get a ride home after calling in sick.

The friend looked out the car window debating what to do.

Then he looked at his watch and realized he would be late if he didn't get moving. He couldn't have a third tardy this month, or he might be fired. He took one last look at his co-worker and called out to him to see if he needed help or if he needed him to call someone but Julien just waved him off. So he put the car in motion and sped towards Baton Rouge. He would never see him again. He got to work anxious as he'd nearly been late and forgot about Julien for a few hours.

# CHAPTER 3

*J*ulien remembered after the friend went down the road that he'd left his work bag and soda behind in the car as he stumbled outside. Oh well, the ginger ale wasn't helping anyway. He really felt awful, ready to heave some more and he was seeing things again. Was that his grandfather down the street? He stumbled straight ahead trying to get closer to images on the horizon, while he squinted against the sun. Man was it bright! He felt his pockets for sunglasses but couldn't find them. He knew he was swaying on his feet and so he wondered what the neighbors might think of his behavior.

After another half block or so, Julien knew that time was running out in more ways than one. He was running out of street, running out of energy as he hadn't dared eat much food in the last six days; he felt like he was running out of time but couldn't focus on where he needed to be.

He was both nauseated and dizzy, one compounding the other. Each step forward felt like he had twenty pounds of mud on each leg. He paused to see a shimmering horizon in front of him.

Was he in the desert? He shook his head as though to clear his vision. No, he wasn't seeing an oasis in the desert, he was in New

13

Orleans and it was a sweltering hot and humid day. It was the city of his birth and re-birth after Hurricane Katrina. He was in the French Quarter he thought. It looked old with wrought iron balconies and he didn't see lots of trees like he'd be in the Garden District. What street was he on? What day was it? What time of day was is? He remembered he thought he hadn't eaten in a while, so maybe it was late afternoon, but where were all the people? The Quarter was always full of tourists.

Covertly, a figure was tailing Mr. Cheval. The man was weaving and stumbling, looking like any other drunk in the French Quarter and therefore he drew little notice from the few early morning people going to work. The figure anticipated the man would drop to the ground in about half a block and he wanted to make sure to direct that fall into an alley. It would take longer in the alley for people to realize that he wasn't sleeping off alcohol and that really, he was dead.

Julien came to a stop holding on to a lamppost squinting at the buildings around him. Was he on Bourbon Street or St. Charles? He looked around for familiar landmarks and saw none. Maybe he should ask for help from the next person passing by him. Surely a stranger wouldn't hurt him? He was sure that people had been following him the last couple of weeks, but if he asked for help from someone walking his way wouldn't that mean they weren't following him?

Again he squinted and watched a woman approach. He was sure he hadn't seen her before so he put a hand out and said something, but she stepped away from him, frowning. He realized that his words had come out slurred. She probably thought he was drunk. He felt drunk and the mud around his legs was making it increasingly hard to lift each foot. Where had the mud come from? He looked at his pants but couldn't see any mud. He held on tighter to the lamppost thinking he might heave. The wave passed and he let go planning on moving down the street until he found an open door. Weren't businesses supposed to be open? All he saw was closed doors and blurring outlines. He found he needed more support and headed for a wall to lean against. He hit it hard with his shoulder misjudging where it actually was. Maybe he'd sit down for a while until he felt better.

The figure watched Mr. Cheval slide down the wall figuring he wouldn't be getting up. He leaned nonchalantly close by trying to decide when he was ready to drag the figure into the alley that was about five feet away. A few people passing him on the street assumed Mr. Cheval was his friend and gave him looks that said 'he needed to find new friends'. He would shrug as they moved past him. When no one was looking, he nudged the man with his shoe and got no response. He waited for a break in potential witnesses and quickly pulled the man the five feet into the slender space between two houses. The man barely roused as the stranger grabbed him by the arms. The killer could tell Mr. Cheval was within an hour of death if he could just die in the peace and quiet of the side yard, then it would be a win for him. After he settled the man behind him, he took up post at the space to block anyone seeing the man lying on the ground. Studying his cell phone he adopted the posture of someone waiting for a ride and killing the time by reading emails.

The time gave him an opportunity to glance around for cameras on the building exteriors and his luck was with him, as Mr. Cheval had wandered down St. Philip Street which was mostly filled with older houses lacking high tech cameras that might have recorded his actions. Kudos to Mr. Cheval for choosing such a convenient place to die thought the man with a small smile on his face. He might not be discovered for a few days if he threw some debris over him.

# CHAPTER 4

$\mathcal{A}$licia Hudson leaned back in her desk chair puzzling over the autopsy results of Julien Cheval. What had killed the young man? He was thin, but hadn't died from starvation or dehydration. His heart was fine, there was no trauma to his body, other than a few rat bites as he'd been chewed on by the local vermin by the time of discovery of his body. At that point, he'd likely been dead for three to four days. His stomach contents were a mess as the decomposition process interfered with the analysis. The toxicology screen showed nothing unusual and no illegal drugs.

She ran her eyes over the folder on her desk checking to see if she missed some fact. The family thought that evil spirits had killed the young man according to the police; Alicia didn't believe in such a thing. She wasn't a native to the Big Easy, New Orleans' nickname. Where she had grown up in Ohio, people had little time for Caribbean religions like Santeria, Kuminia, or Voodoo. These folk religions believed in some degree of magic for everyday occurrences. Alicia had been raised in a Christian faith and all of her science training for medical school had taught her to have no faith in magic.

She sat there scratching her head and pulling on her long red hair. How did she rule this death? Her training aimed her toward 'undetermined'. She hated using that term and usually fought to find an absolute ruling in a death. She thought about asking her fellow pathologists for their opinions, but they were natives to the area and were at times intellectually lazy and likely willing to swallow the claim of evil spirits so they could move on to the next case. Alicia knew her supervisor, the coroner of New Orleans would want her to move on. He wasn't a pathologist by training but instead had been elected as the coroner from a law enforcement background. He lacked the medical education for her to consult with him on the technicalities of the deceased.

Who else could she ask for help? She was tired as she had been mulling over the case in her head while tossing and turning last night. She looked up and caught one of the plaques on her wall showing her completing her medical training in pathology in a hospital in Southern California. She thought back to her training days and the other residents she trained with. She respected all of them and they had kept in touch during the first five years after their fellowships and then drifted apart to different parts of the United States. She began looking at her training partners to see if any of them were in the southern part of the United States. None were. She looked at what some of her classmates were doing and then lingered over Jill Quint. They had enjoyed each other's company during training and then she began reading about Jill. Wow, she had solved some unusual cases and now she worked as a consultant according to her website. She'd be perfect for this job, but she knew the coroner wouldn't support paying an outside expert on this case. She felt strongly about getting an answer for this man. Jill was always a good sport and loved intrigue. Maybe she would consult for free if she could offer her a free plane ride that she would pay for and offer her a bedroom in her house? She had nothing to lose by asking so she picked up the phone and made the call.

Jill was outside in her vineyard trimming the vines as they

were beginning to lose their leaves due to fall. She heard her phone ring and pulled it out to look at it; her phone indicated that the call was from New Orleans. Jill debated answering as she'd been getting a lot of robot calls recently. Then she decided to answer as most robot call computers gave up after the third ring.

"This is Jill Quint."

"Hi Jill, it's Alicia Hudson."

Jill's brain in a matter of milliseconds traveled from her vineyard back to her medical school days, "You're a voice from the past and now you're in New Orleans or at least that's what my phone says. Are you working as a pathologist for Jefferson Parish?"

Alicia chuckled remembering Jill's tendency to combine several thoughts into a few sentences. Yes, it was the same old Jill.

"Yes I am. How about you? How's the consulting business?"

There was a laugh on the other end of the phone as Jill replied, "Either my life is in danger or I'm in my vineyard cutting dead shoots off my grapevines."

"Those are some extremes," Alicia replied with a grin in her voice. "So you own a vineyard? Are you producing wine yet and if so what's the name?"

"I bought a vineyard six years ago and I'm in my second year of production and you wouldn't have heard of me as I've only sold locally, but the name is Quixotic Winery. How are you enjoying New Orleans? The weather's a far cry from Southern California."

"It took a while to get used to the humidity and walking in and out of air conditioning all day. I think I spent the first six months dealing with inflamed allergies from air conditioning and mold, but now I'm used to it. There are a bunch of cultural things that people do in this region that I enjoy and the people are nice and friendly."

"So I'm thinking you called me for a reason. What can I do for you?"

"I have a body in my morgue and I've been unable to account

for his death. The family says that evil spirits took him over and killed him. Since I don't recall a chapter in our residency about 'death by evil spirits', I've looked for a more solid explanation and haven't found one."

"That sounds intriguing. How old is he, where was he found dead, and what were your unusual findings?"

"He's thirty-three, he was found in an alley in the residential area of the French Quarter. There are no markings on his body and his tox screen came back clear. I'd like to fly you to New Orleans, but my budget won't pay for anything more than your flight here. You could stay with me. Doesn't that sound more interesting than pruning grapevines?"

Jill laughed at her final comment and had to admit she was right; she loved a good mystery. She had no consulting jobs on the horizon, but then usually she didn't have more than one job a month and it was last minute calls like this one that often brought her into cases.

"You know Alicia, your case sounds interesting and your terms are satisfactory. Let me check out a few things here and get back to you in say, an hour. Okay?"

"That great news! What's been your oddest death case so far?"

"I've had nothing but odd cases and remind me to tell you about them when I arrive."

"Okay; look forward to talking to you in an hour," Alicia said as they ended the call. Alicia thought that it sounded like Jill was mostly convinced to come.

Jill looked around the vineyard for Trixie, her Dalmatian dog as usually she could see the dog's spots through the vines. After her second 360 degree turn, she spotted the dog digging a hole. She sighed and walked through the vineyard to the dog looking for evidence of rodents, but didn't see any.

"Com'on Trixie girl, let's go get some lunch while mom figures out if she should fly to Louisiana."

Looking at her schedule for the next few days, she picked up the phone to call Nathan, her partner of the past three years.

"Hey babe, how's it going?" she heard him ask.

"I'm enjoying the dullness of pruning vines."

"Sure beats avoiding being pushed over a castle wall," referring to her most recent case in Scotland.

"Exactly my thought! Hey I just got a phone call from an old classmate in New Orleans and she would like my help on a case. I was the Chief Resident during her first year of residency, then I stayed on and did further training in toxicology so our paths crossed a lot over those two years. I like the context of the problem in NOLA," a nickname for New Orleans. "A young man was found dead and his family believes that evil spirits killed him. I'd love to dispel that kind of theory."

"Really? Evil spirits? Even I, as a completely non-medical person, would find that hard to swallow as the cause of death. Does your old college friend believe that?"

"Not in the least, but she hates to label the death as 'unde-termined'."

"So you're going to go. Will Angela, Marie, and Jo be joining you?"

"No, she can only afford my flight. No per-Diem day rate, no hotel – she plans to put me up at her house."

"Wow, that's two unpaid jobs in a row. Not a great way to grow your business!"

"Fortunately, as a world famous vintner I can afford a few unpaid jobs," Jill said with irony in her voice.

"Hey don't be hard on yourself, you doubled your grape production this year and you've already sold out!" Nathan replied knowing the details of Jill's vineyard.

"Yeah, at least I'm making a tiny profit now instead of pulling on my savings. Yes, it is a bummer that my time won't be paid, but if I can figure out the cause of death, at least it will bulk up my resume and perhaps give me a reputation in the southern United States."

"If you're there longer than three days, I'll join you. There are some interesting distilleries there and I would like to view their marketing."

Jill thought for a moment of the Caribbean influence on the area and asked, "Rum?"

"Yes, and gin and vodka."

"That sounds interesting."

"Yeah, like I said they have some interesting marketing to attract people as you don't naturally associate vodka with New Orleans. You want me to watch Trixie? If I decide later to come then I'll give Lucy a call and see if she's available to care for Arthur and Trixie," Nathan said referring to his cat.

"Sounds like a plan. Let's have dinner tonight and I'll leave Trixie with you. I'll leave early in the morning for NOLA."

She ended the call with Nathan and put in a call to Alicia.

She answered the call with "You're going to come!"

"Yes, the challenge is too great not to want to get to the bottom of an evil spirits diagnosis. I'll leave early in the morning and arrive at about five. Can you pick me up?"

"It's the least I can do," Alicia replied excited to renew her acquaintance with Jill and have a trusted colleague on this case.

"Also if you could send me your reports including pictures at the scene, I'll be able to review them before I get there. I have a mini-forensic lab on my property and if a case is close by, I'll fly home with specimens to process them, but NOLA is too far away. What's your lab capacity there?"

"Actually, it's pretty good. We have a couple of medical schools, Tulane and LSU in NOLA, and LSU has a branch up the road in Shreveport. They would likely love to help with the case and I know some of the professors there so if you have something unusual, they would join us in solving this mystery."

"Excellent! Then I think we're all set," Jill said passing on her flight information for Alicia's department to book.

# CHAPTER 5

*J*ill looked around her lab for useful things she could use in this case. She wouldn't be processing tissue samples herself and in the end, she couldn't think of anything unique to take to NOLA, so early the next morning she was on her way to the airport for her connection to Los Angeles and on to New Orleans. She'd dropped an email to her part-time teammates Jo, Marie, and Angela explaining the case and the lack of payment. Marie and Angela offered to help how they could without traveling to NOLA, Jo mentioned she would be arriving in two days for a convention and would have some evening downtime so she could help. Jill arranged to have dinner with Jo on her first night. As Jo was coming from Wisconsin she had a much shorter trip and fewer time zones than Jill.

As promised, Alicia was waiting for Jill upon arrival in NOLA. They went to the arts district to a Mexican restaurant that featured a NOLA version of Mexican food and cucumber daiquiris and Jill liked NOLA immediately despite the humidity. Jill usually avoided spicy food, but found her taste buds did just fine with Cajun flavoring in her chicken tacos. As for the cucumber daiquiris, she thought she could drink four or five of them they were so delicious, smooth, and cool to the taste.

"Do you eat here often?" Jill asked.

"Yeah, it represents the crossroads of Southern California and New Orleans. There are many fabulous restaurants here, but you know me - I was never a foodie so it's wasted on me. I prefer the great food here and I also like po'boy sandwiches and the beignets at Café Du Monde. Even though it's a tourist attraction, the donuts are great."

"I have to agree with you there. I'm not a foodie either primarily because there are many ingredients in things that I don't care to eat like onions and mushrooms. I'm thinking the chef at the Commander's Palace might have difficulty meeting my needs. It's just easier to eat simpler foods."

"Besides I'd rather put my salary into my mortgage than dine out every night."

They continued to talk for a while on the difference between Southern California and New Orleans. Eventually, they circled back to the reason that Jill had come to New Orleans.

"Tell me about your set-up here. I imagine your coroner's office is old," Jill said.

"Actually, it was rebuilt after Hurricane Katrina so it's state of the art. I arrived after it was built. I understand the old coroner's office was an old mortuary with lots of mold and a tendency to flood with heavy rain and there were refrigerator trucks in a parking lot to hold the remains."

"Wow, that sounds like something from a previous century."

"I heard that part of the problem was the elected coroner at the time never asked for additional resources. He was uncomfortable with the political side of his job. All I know is that we have great working conditions now and no refrigerated trailers holding the deceased."

"In my travels as a consultant, I've come across some scary bad coroner offices. Mostly, they're small, poor towns with an elected coroner who has no medical background. If that's the case then they care more about pleasing the mortuary in town than doing a thorough death investigation."

Alicia paid their bill and they headed into the Irish Channel area of New Orleans. She had a small and old house in the shotgun style with touches of Victorian Gingerbread. Beige on the outside with white trim and a small front patio, it was full of cuteness. She showed Jill into her guest bedroom explaining a little of the architecture style as they walked.

"This house dates back to about 1900. The plumbing and electrical were updated before I bought it as well as some additions for modern times like larger closets. I'm saving for central air, but in the interim, you'll have a window unit."

"Sounds like you plan on staying a while," Jill said.

"I lived in many cities as you know and yet I find it charming here and I like the pace of life, so yes, I guess I'll be staying," Alicia said with a smile.

"It's good to put down roots. When I worked for the state, I always felt like I was on the paperwork and court testifying circuit. I didn't like it. If you're ever in the San Francisco area, I'm about ninety minutes out depending on traffic," Jill said making a face. "I love my home and vineyard and they bring me peace after some tough consultant cases."

"We'll have a lot of time to talk while you're here but just tell me about your most unusual death."

"Unusual because it's a rare way to die, or unusual as far as autopsy findings?"

"Wow, the fact that you can ask me that question says that you've seen a vast array of strange cases. I'm glad I was able to talk you into coming here."

"My friend, Nathan who is an artist said that even he knew you couldn't die by evil spirits, so your case will likely be added to my list of weird ways to die."

"So back to your question, for now tell me the most unusual way to die."

Jill thought through her cases and decided she wasn't ready to talk about Nick being pushed off the castle tower, so she settled for, "Fake paramedics arrive saying that your pacemaker is sending out alerts that it's malfunctioning and then they electrocute you with over-juiced paddles."

Alicia stood there with her mouth open for a few seconds, then shut it and swallowed. All she could say was "Wow". And then after a moment she added, "I'm glad I thought of you and you were willing to donate your time. You must have expertise way beyond the average pathologist."

"Let's just say I don't get called into cases where someone watches someone else shoot someone dead."

"Okay, I'm going to ply you with cucumber daiquiris while you're my housemate so I can hear some of your stories. I also hope to learn from you tomorrow when we review the remains of Mr. Cheval."

"I'm sure you did a great job since I was your Chief Resident at one time," Jill said with a smile. "Besides from everything I looked over on my flight here it seems like you did a very thorough examination. My guess is that there's a toxin that hasn't come to light yet. Can you arrange an appointment with the family for tomorrow? I think that will help us move beyond the usual suspects to something very rare. You don't just die at such a young age without a cause. Even if he'd been shot with a curare dart, you would have seen the evidence. It wasn't cold here so exposure is out of the question. His skin didn't seem to exhibit the signs of extreme dehydration as a cause either. His heart muscle was fine and he didn't blow a major artery in his heart or brain."

Alicia had been listening and nodding as Jill went through common causes of death, and said, "So I think we're back to a poison of some sort or evil spirits."

"Somehow I must have missed that disease classification in

medical school as I've never seen or heard of death by evil spirits," Jill said. "However, I'm in a culturally very different part of America and I don't mean to make fun of people's beliefs. I'm sure the family is an otherwise rational group of people except when it comes to the death of Mr. Cheval."

"There are many obscure poisons out there, how do we narrow the list and then test for them?" Alicia asked.

"I think that is where the family will help. I think we need to know a lot more about the man. Who talked to the family?"

"The police; his mother said he died by evil spirits and I gather the investigators didn't get much beyond that explanation."

"I think they thought he was just another casualty of alcohol poisoning even though I've never seen a case in a man so young and black. Alcohol poisoning almost always occurs in older Caucasians in Louisiana."

"Have the police finished their investigation?" Jill asked.

"Yes. There were no findings from the autopsy for them to follow up on."

"Was the young man a native of New Orleans? Where does his mom get the evil spirits idea?"

"Yes he was born in this city."

"Tell me about the origin of evil spirits in New Orleans," Jill said.

"What do you mean the origin of evil spirits? Personally, I try to avoid evil people," Alicia said not understanding Jill's question.

"I mean the concept of 'evil spirits' has to originate somewhere. It's not something that someone would say in Los Angeles so it must be culturally related to this area. Is it a religion or an ethnic group?"

"Oh, now I get your question. I've only lived here about two years and haven't had the time to explore some of the more obscure parts of the city including understanding Voodoo and Hoodoo. Heck they call NOLA the most haunted city in America, but I've yet to experience any ghosts at home or work."

"So Voodoo and Hoodoo are not just tourists attractions; they are a religion for a certain group of people here?" Jill asked trying to understand the two terms.

"You know," Alicia said thinking, "someone in my office practices voodoo. Let me call Sylviane and see if she's doing anything. We could meet her somewhere for a drink."

Alicia grabbed her cellphone checking the time. Eight was a little late to call and ask for information, but she could always turn them down. She dialed the number and had a short conversation from what Jill could hear from her side of the conversation. She ended the call and said, "Let's go, she's going to meet us at a bar on Magazine Street so it's not too far from here and we can walk if you like."

"Yes let's walk. I always feel like I sit for hours when I travel. What does Sylviane do for your office?"

"She's a mortuary aid."

"Ah," Jill said knowing that meant the woman went on scene to pick up the deceased and performed duties like tagging clothing and other personal effects and took the weight of an incoming human. Bodies could be in a state of awful decomposition at the time the mortuary aid was called to remove remains.

They had a four block walk and Jill could already feel the humidity in the perspiration drops that ran down her spine. The air felt moist and green like she was smelling plants whose names she didn't know, but they had no particular fragrance other than green. She loved walking the streets as you learned more about a city like the smell of green. They soon reached Magazine Street and Jill was charmed by the myriad of small restaurants, bars, and businesses.

They came to a stop outside what looked like a house, but the sign on the door indicated it was a tavern. Alicia opened the door and they entered a long narrow room with beautiful wooden ceilings, panels, and a bar. Alicia walked up to the woman from work. She was black, with short coiffed hair and a friendly smile. Alicia asked if they wanted wine and so she ordered a bottle and three glasses and they went outside to a tiny patio that was empty. There no one would be able to hear their conversation. It wasn't a secret or confidential, Alicia just wanted the freedom for them without strangers listening in.

After introductions were completed Jill asked, "As Alicia mentioned, I'm here consulting on a death that the family says is due to evil spirits. I'd like to understand what evil spirits are and who worries about them in this city."

Sylviane laughed at Jill's question and said, "Don't you worry about evil spirits in your life?"

"Ah, no. Of all the bad things that have happened to me in my life, I've had a role in causing them. I worry more about self-stupidity or self-centeredness causing me to miss clues about the world around me."

"Perhaps then since you're such a pragmatic person you have trouble understanding the culture here. I practice voodoo and I'm also Catholic."

"Catholic? I thought Voodoo involved the worship of something other than God," Jill asked.

"Many people in New Orleans have roots in West Africa or the Caribbean and so Voodoo is a melting pot of those cultures with that of Native Americans from this region. So at the heart we believe in the visible and non-visible world. We're sitting in the visible world, but once my grandmother died she went to the invisible world."

"Is your invisible world heaven?"

"Yes in a way, but to a practitioner of Voodoo it perhaps feels a lot more tangible as we can look at the world around us and feel the love of our forefathers. It also gives us a focus on the community. We want both worlds to be happy and do better," Sylviane explained.

"Do you have evil spirits?" Jill asked.

"We have spirits that create mischief which can test your

patience, but we don't recognize bad or evil spirits as the work of the devil."

"Are you aware of an African or Caribbean group of people that worry about evil spirits?"

"Perhaps you're not putting the term in context. Did the family say the deceased was killed by evil spirits, did his body contain evil spirits, or was the family saying that the murderer must be filled with evil spirits?"

"Good point Sylviane," Alicia said. "I haven't spoken with the family yet so I'll get that clarified tomorrow. You've been a big help, thanks for coming out at this late hour to chat with us."

"You're welcome. There are so many misconceptions about Voodoo that I try to clear the air whenever possible. I'll give my auntie a call when I get home to see if she knows of any local religions that might fear evil spirits."

While they finished sipping their wine they moved on to a discussion of strange cases each had seen. Sylviane volunteered the story of a middle age man killed by fire ants.

"I was terrified when we went to retrieve the body that the ants would come after us, but they had an exterminator spray the area first. Still, I was constantly checking my body over the slightest itch. When we returned to the office, I quickly hosed the victim down, then went and got a shower and incinerated my clothing as well as his. I wanted to be sure the bugs were very dead."

All the women shuddered at that story and Jill asked, "Did you have nightmares that first night?"

"No I went to church, and then I went home and ate a big meal washed down with nearly an entire bottle of wine. I was fairly sure that the carbohydrates and wine would put me into a coma to sleep and it did."

"That's an excellent solution. With the big meal you would hopefully not wake up hung over the next day," Jill suggested.

"Exactly, I was fine the next day."

Alicia offered her strange case. "I had a female that had been sawed apart by her husband and placed in the freezer. Since it was obvious what killed the woman, I looked for evidence that he hadn't done it to her while she was alive. Fortunately, from her perspective, he shot her in the head first. He actually sawed her into gallon freezer bag pieces; so for the family's sake, I made sure I had all of the baggies containing her remains. It took me a few hours to assemble all the parts and make sure she was all there."

Again the women commiserated on the awfulness of the case and they were expecting Jill to tell a story. She was sorting through her memory on what was the most disgusting of her cases. She didn't have a story to match theirs, and so told this story, "There was a woman in Antwerp that I tried to save from a peanut-induced allergic shock reaction. She made it alive to the hospital with a friend and I doing CPR in an ambulance but then the murderer slipped in the hospital emergency room and sat her up which the heart can't handle after all the epinephrine we gave her to counter the anaphylaxis. The Belgium doctor that performed her autopsy found diamonds in her stomach which was an interesting case."

"What was the value of those diamonds?" Alicia asked.

"I have no idea," Jill said with a laugh. "But the stomach was unusually heavy and that's what made the pathologist look inside."

Alicia looked at Sylviane and said, "Why don't we get those kinds of cases - where the patient pays us as we cut them open?"

"Well, I've only had one of those in my life," Jill said.

"Yes but imagine the value of say half a pound of diamonds," Alicia fantasized searching for something on her cellphone. "This website says it would be about eight and a half million dollars. Yep, I could retire on those stomach contents."

"Except you would have to turn them over to the police," Jill reminded her. "Wouldn't you agree that anyone found with half a pound of diamonds in their stomach must be related to a criminal case? There's no reason to swallow diamonds unless you're trying to hide them and it only works for a short time as you would poop them out in say twenty-four hours."

"Yuck," Sylviane said.

"If I knew there was even a chance of one-hundred-thousand dollars of diamonds in a pile of poop, I'd search," Alicia said. "Certainly compared to a corpse with maggots in it, it couldn't be any grosser."

"We sound like a bunch of ten-year-old boys trying to gross each other out," Jill said with a laugh.

Sylviane stood up and said, "I have to get up in eight hours to go work tomorrow so I'd better head home. I'm thinking I'll see both of you there tomorrow."

Jill and Alicia went back the way they came. The evening was still warm, but she could get a glimpse of the average citizen of New Orleans through the lit windows as they passed homes on their way.

# CHAPTER 6

*J*ill and Alicia were standing over Mr. Cheval. He was laid out on a stainless steel table in a brightly lit room. Windows gave them natural light which was better for an autopsy. The table tilted slightly downhill so that fluids drained away from the body. The usual scale was nearby as was a microphone suspended from the ceiling for dictation. There was room for two other autopsies to take place.

Jill had a quick tour before they examined Mr. Cheval. The office had a nice cooler to store the unclaimed dead. They also had a good specimen room filled with large pickle jars containing organs, eyes, and tissues, so they could go back and run tests if necessary. Their supply area carried the routine toxicology kits containing various size bottles to run tests and these were tracked as evidence with paperwork documenting the chain of custody. Alicia mentioned they sent their kits to St. Louis and there was normally a five to nine-week turnaround to get results. She'd put a priority on Mr. Cheval because of his age and the lack of an obvious cause of death.

The two pathologists walked through Alicia's autopsy. Jill could find no new findings from Alicia's autopsy. The lack of physical findings was extremely rare. Next, they examined the personal possessions the man arrived with. The fact that his body had sat out in the warm ambient air for a few days did little for the aroma of the clothing. Jill was glad for the hepa filter mask which served to decrease some of the odor. Given that his body had leaked fluids as had the ground he'd been found on, it was difficult to figure out what stains created which potential evidence.

"Was any of his clothing sampled?"

"I don't believe so; let me check the police report," Alicia said spending a few moments looking at the report. Then she turned around and said "no".

Jill looked around the room and saw lab analyzers collecting dust and asked Alicia, "Why don't you run your specimens here? This looks like new equipment."

"This building was part of the reconstruction after Hurricane Katrina. The city, and parishes were given money to replace buildings lost in the storm. As a part of the building plans, we were outfitted with analyzers but weren't given the staff to operate the machinery. So the equipment is new and hasn't ever been used."

"Do you have supplies for the equipment?"

"Supplies?" Alicia questioned.

"Kits to calibrate the machines, specimen tubes that each machine uses etc. I have these same analyzers in my home lab. I can run the specimens for you here. You might not want to use those results in a court of law, but they might clue us in as to what killed Mr. Cheval."

"Oh okay. Let me look and I'll ask Sylviane if she's seen anything."

Jill said, "Let me help search. I know what I'm looking for."

They spent the next half hour searching for supplies for the analyzers. They were able to locate a few kits for each machine, all expired. Jill did a scientific search on Google and decided it wasn't a good idea to use the expired kits. Alicia checked in with a pathologist friend at one of the city's hospitals and was able to arrange to borrow the kits. Meanwhile, since Jill had a supply in her California lab, Nathan would overnight them to NOLA to replace those they borrowed.

"Wow, like every twenty minutes I find a new reason to be glad you're helping me with this case. You are beyond resourceful," Alicia said.

Jill felt a little embarrassed that she was able to do more with her home lab than this big city lab could do in terms of turn-around time.

"We may find nothing after all of this effort to get those machines running," Jill cautioned. "Remember you'll get the same results in five to eight weeks from St. Louis. So your victim was still getting the same excellent examination from you, I'm just speeding that up."

"After I'm done with this case, I'm going to get certified in those analyzers so I can run the tests myself like you do. The cost of the kits compared to the cost of sending specimens to St Louis would be less and we would get results faster. There are still some tests that we will have to send out, but I think I could do away with perhaps eighty percent of them. I wonder how my fellow pathologists will feel about running the analyzers?"

"Some will agree with your approach, others will say it's beneath them. You might be able to train your mortuary assistants to run the equipment knowing that regardless the lab is not certified no matter who does it and specimen results needed for the court would still have to be sent out, but that's probably a small amount of the specimens in this lab."

"Let's see how it goes with this case, then I'll formulate a proposal to my fellow pathologists before taking the matter to our coroner. If we might be able to cut costs by screening in-house he would be all for it. We'll see."

"Let's run over to the hospital and get those kits before they change their minds. Then we can decide what we want to run here especially in regards to the clothing."

"Let's go," agreed Alicia.

An hour later they were back in the morgue carrying a box of kits. Jill pulled covers off the machinery and cleaned the dust. She'd powered them up before they left in case any of the analyzers had long computer warm-ups. She looked at the equipment and then her watch and said, "I think we'll be a while getting this equipment going and deciding our testing process. Aren't we due to talk to the family soon?"

"Oh my gosh, I feel like a kid in a candy shop with you Jill. Yes, we're due there in twenty minutes. They live in the Ninth Ward. Let's go."

# CHAPTER 7

$\mathcal{A}$licia used her phone's GPS to find the house belonging to Mr. Cheval's mother. It was the first time Jill had seen the damage wrought by Hurricane Katrina. It was shocking to see more than twelve years later that there were still houses with watermarks on them. She wondered how the homes were still livable. There were empty concrete slabs everywhere. Where had the people gone?

"Did any of your current pathologists work during Katrina? I would think that it would be a nightmare to have sorted through all of those dead bodies especially given that so many had water damage."

"They don't talk about it. I know that in addition to the misery of the storm, then the misery of the deaths, there were another one hundred forty or so bodies that floated out of their burial sites. They had coroners from across the country helping with identification and I'm not sure they ever identified them all. As you can see beyond the tourist areas, there is still damage from Katrina that hasn't been fixed. The human stories are terrible. There was one of many families profiled where home ownership passed down the family and no one ever took the time to update the records at the parish. So Grandma Jones who died thirty years ago is still the registered owner and now the children can't get government money to make repairs or rebuild their house. It's really sad."

"Yes, it has a feel to it of being deserted by the rest of America," Jill said. "Are they rebuilding homes that will be flooded by the next hurricane?"

"The Army Corps of Engineers rebuilt the levees and made them higher so they should withstand another large hurricane. They also are making an effort to restore the wetlands as those help prevent storm surge. Let's hope they got it right. If you have ten to fifteen thousand dollars, you can buy a lot here and plant another vineyard."

Jill looked out the window as they traveled down streets, amazed to see signs of optimism on some streets and bleak despair on others. "I don't think that would work, my vines would rot here as the ground is so moist. Grapes really like dry heat."

Shortly they pulled up in front of a two-story house that looked well maintained.

Alicia looked at the house and said, "This is a house that was refurbished after the hurricane. It's a little farther from the canal and the foundation is higher although not as high as some built recently. The newer construction has a parking space below the house and it's on stilts."

They walked up to the front door and rang the doorbell, a black woman in her fifties or sixties answered the door. She looked like she'd been crying. This had to be the victim's mother.

"Mrs. Cheval? I'm Dr. Hudson and this is Dr. Quint from the coroner's office."

She nodded and opened the door wider inviting them in.

"Would you like a cup of tea?" asked Mrs. Cheval.

Jill hated tea but followed Alicia's lead on southern manners.

Alicia nodded and said, "Thank you for the offer, we would love some."

She left the room and Alicia whispered, "I bet she's making a drink called sweet tea here in the south. If you still have that sweet tooth, you'll love it."

They looked around the living room while they waited and noticed several family pictures. Jill didn't want to be caught staring at a picture of the man they just cut open. Fortunately, Mrs. Cheval returned to the room holding the tea tray.

She poured a cup and passed it to Jill first and then Alicia. Then there was silence.

Alicia cleared her throat and said, "As I mentioned on the phone, I'm puzzled by your son's death. I don't have evidence to rule on the mode of death. I've asked a second pathologist to examine my work and help me with the case. Dr. Quint is from California."

Jill spoke for the first time and said, "I'm sorry for your loss Mrs. Cheval and I know this is a bad time for you, but we wanted some more information about your son to understand his death."

"Thank you," nodded Mrs. Cheval.

"First can you tell me something about your family? Can you tell me if your parents and siblings are alive and if so their ages and any health problems. Also, I understand you have a grandson, can you tell me his age and about his health. If any of our questions seem too personal, we mean no disrespect, we're simply looking for clues in our investigation."

"My parents perished during Katrina like many elderly in this neighborhood. They were stubborn and didn't believe the warnings. We found their bodies when the waters receded. We found them together in what was left of their house. They were seventy and seventy-two and both took medication for high blood pressure but were otherwise in good health. I have nine brothers and sisters and three are suffering from diabetes. I'm going on two years as a breast cancer survivor. My grandson is seven and he's in good health, a smart and strong boy. He's been staying with his mama since shortly before Julien died."

Jill observed there was nothing unusual in this family's health history other than the tragedy of Katrina.

"Did your grandson normally stay with his mother or did he spend time with you and his father?"

"I would say that Julien had Jayden, that's my grandson's name, about one-third of the time. He and Jayden's mother have a cooperative sharing arrangement and since Julien lived here, I've also helped raise Jayden. He's a good boy." There was joy and love in Mrs. Cheval's face when she spoke of her grandson.

Then she added, "Julien had something bothering him for the past three months or so, but he wouldn't tell me what it was. This last month his anxiety really started climbing. He was spooked, and he lost weight. Then last week he moved Jayden to his mama's house; he said it wasn't safe for him here. At times he seemed to hallucinate, but then he'd be fine by Sunday evening. He went to work Monday and when he got home from work, he wouldn't eat, he just lay down in his bedroom. I called Father Jules as he knew Julien as I didn't know what to do. I thought Julien was in spiritual pain as he wouldn't tell me what was wrong."

"What kind of hallucinations did he have? Was he seeing people or things? Do you have any sense of when they started and stopped?" Jill asked, thinking about toxins.

Mrs. Cheval thought about her question and then responded, "If I didn't know better, I would have said he was taking one of those sixties drugs LSD or something, he was seeing bugs and people shortly after he got home from work. They would go away by the end of the evening and his brain would be back and focused the next morning before he left for work."

Both Alicia and Jill started to ask questions at the same time, and Alicia deferred to Jill as her guest, "So it seemed to you that something was making him sick at work which would wear off in time?"

She nodded and said, "I asked him about it."

"What was his job?" Jill asked.

"He was an agriculture inspector so he worked mostly in the field inspecting farmer stuff in the state."

Her explanation gave the two pathologists a range of additional diseases and conditions that might have struck him if he was around livestock.

"Did you ever talk or text with him mid-day? Do you know if he felt okay at lunch?" Jill asked.

"Some days he did and some days he didn't. I thought it must be connected to the weather as he felt worse on hot days."

Alicia and Jill were taking notes as fast as they could, their minds swiftly adding to a list of potential causes of death.

"Did he drive his vehicle or did the state provide him with one?"

"He drove a state vehicle as it carried gadgets that he needed to do his job. In fact, the truck is still here - it's parked behind the house."

"Do you have the keys to it?" Jill asked.

"No, at least I haven't searched Julien's room for them as no one has asked me for the keys. After you leave, I'll make sure I locate them."

The two pathologists could tell that the woman was barely holding it together and no wonder given she'd recently suffered the death of her son. Alicia reached over and offered the woman a second cup of her own tea.

She briefly smiled her thanks and took a few moments to regain her composure. Jill stood up and looked out the window giving the mother privacy. She also looked through the room that must have been the kitchen to the utility type truck parked beyond that window.

Mrs. Cheval signaled that they could resume questioning and Jill returned to the seating area.

"Mrs. Cheval, would you mind if we took a look at that truck after we finish our conversation here?" Jill asked. She nodded her agreement and they moved on to other questions.

"Your son was found in a residential area of the French Quarter, is there an agricultural area close to that area? Did he have a work-related reason to be there and since his truck is parked here, how did he get there?" Alicia asked understanding Jill's process for asking questions.

"He wasn't feeling well that day and so he called his friend Keith to see if he could get a ride to work. Keith said he started feeling nauseated as he drove him to Baton Rouge and asked to be let out of his car in the French Quarter. Keith was anxious for Julien, but he also didn't want him throwing up inside his car. Julien told him he was just stepping out to get a drink of bottled water and he would find another way to get back home, so the friend drove on as he didn't want to be late himself."

"When did you realize there was something wrong?" Alicia asked.

"I didn't know about Julien getting out of the car until later that night. He didn't come home and so I called Keith and spoke with him about that morning and he gave me the location of where he'd dropped Julien off. He offered to take me over to the location that evening and so we found ourselves knocking on doors around the area where he got out of the car, but no one had seen him. I called the police but they wouldn't take a report as he was an adult and he hadn't been missing twenty-four hours yet. I told them he'd been sick, but they still refused to take a report."

Alicia looked at her notes and then said, "Was that Monday evening?" Today was Friday.

"Yes, I went back to the police after the twenty-four hour mark and filed a report on Tuesday. He was found Wednesday."

As Alicia had done the autopsy Wednesday afternoon, she knew he'd been found Wednesday morning.

With tears in her voice she murmured, "He was only discovered because it was garbage day and the residents saw him when they approached their garbage cans to put them at the curb. He might have laid there for a week if it hadn't been garbage day on

Wednesday. He had identification on him and so the police came calling to my house. Clearly, from their attitude, they thought he was just another alcohol-related death in the French Quarter. They were skeptical that he'd been on his way to work."

Jill and Alicia waited a few moments to give Mrs. Cheval a chance to regain her composure.

"Can you tell me more about your son's symptoms?" Jill asked.

"It started slowly perhaps two months ago? Julien came home from work feeling nauseous. As time passed, he felt a whole lot more nauseous to the point that I heard him throwing up some nights. Perhaps a week before his death, he started hallucinating in the evening. Often times when he came in from his truck, he would stumble, nearly falling. If I didn't know better I would say he had too much to drink, but I couldn't smell alcohol on his breath and he swore he hadn't drunk any alcohol."

"Tell me more about the hallucinations. Was he seeing things that were not there? Was he seeing people in the room who weren't there? While he was hallucinating was he happy or scared or angry?" Jill asked.

Julien's mom took a few moments to think about her son over the past couple of weeks. She replied as though thinking out loud while she spoke, "Julien has always been a genuinely happy man and so I would say that the hallucinations must have been mostly happy experiences for him because he didn't seem afraid or angry. As for the actual hallucinations, he was either seeing dead people or flowers sometimes."

"What do you mean by dead people? Relatives or friends that you have lost? Or perhaps people that look like they belong in a zombie movie?" Jill asked.

"He saw his grandparents and one of my brothers that died during Katrina. As a family, we follow the Catholic faith, but we also believe in voodoo with the second world of our dead relatives around us in the environment. Some people say there's a fine line between feeling the presence of our departed ones and thinking that we've actually seen them as we go about our day."

Alicia said, "Yes I understand what you're saying Mrs. Cheval. There's a woman in my office who also practices voodoo and that's exactly how she explained it so I can see the difficulty when the hallucinations first set as to whether your son was feeling the presence of deceased family members or did he actually believe they were in the living room with him."

"Exactly."

While they were talking, Jill had been sifting through a variety of poisons and their symptoms in her head. Some poisons were hard to find on testing, while others were hard to find because they were rarely used to commit murder. She had one last question for Mrs. Cheval.

"The police indicated in their report that you believed that evil spirits had killed your son. Can you explain what you mean by that statement?"

"My son was a good person and a good father. You would have to be an evil person with an evil spirit to have ended his life. If you're asking me if I believe in evil charms or witch doctors, or that my deceased relatives have come back to life the answer is no. Until I go to heaven I won't be reunited with my son," Mrs. Cheval said with finality and tears in her voice.

# CHAPTER 8

Alicia and Jill were discussing their conversation on the way back to the coroner's office.

"That was a good lesson for me. I can't believe all the useful information from the victim's mother we received. I wonder why the police misinterpreted her statement about evil spirits?" mused Alicia.

"I always find it very helpful to talk to the family members of the deceased, but I'd be the first to admit it's very draining of one's spirit. You generally learn more about what a good soul that person was and you feel for the friends and family left behind. I think when I worked for the state Medical Examiner's Office, I lacked that perspective on many cases. We were pushed to keep up with our workload and in probably ninety-five percent of the work I did, there was absolutely zero mystery as to how and why a person died; so talking to the family didn't impact the paperwork that we had to complete with each case. I think that now that I'm a consultant, I only end up with that rare one percent of weird death cases."

"The more the mother talked, the more I kept switching directions on which poison might have a role in Julien's death."

"Yeah, I was doing the same thing. It was like a Rolodex was flipping inside my brain each with a different flash card of the particular poison. Another issue for me is I'm not familiar with this part of the country and the plants that are native here. There might be a whole set of poisonous plants on the Gulf Coast that I haven't seen before," Jill said.

"If it makes you feel better I've never had a body in my morgue killed by an exotic plant poison. I think we should start with the run-of-the-mill drugs. I wonder if LSD is still available for purchase on the street? Usually, if people die of a drug overdose in New Orleans, it's either heroin or methamphetamine. Maybe I'll put a question to the narcotics squad and see if there are any new street drugs that might've produced these effects."

"Some of those analyzers in your lab will do some chemical analysis and that may give us a clue as well," Jill said and then added, "Stop the car, I want to go back and sample the work truck to see if there's anything odd in or about it. We don't have a search warrant to do this and the state will wake up on someday and remember that the vehicle is here and will remove it back to the work location. So let's strike while the iron is hot!"

A few short moments later they were back at the Cheval house notifying Mrs. Cheval that they were going to take a few minutes to examine Julien's work truck. She passed them the keys she'd found and waved them back signaling her agreement.

The truck looked like a standard issue work pick-up truck. The bed of the truck had odds and ends in it at both sides had locked storage spaces. There was room on top to store ladders, cords, or hoses. The state seal was on the side of the door. The interior of the cab was generally clean with papers on the seat. Jill tried the locked compartments first to see if they were locked and they were. Fortunately, she carried specimen containers so they could sample the various surfaces of the truck.

Jill took a swipe at the dashboard and steering wheel and the driver side air vent. She also sampled each of the locked compartments though she had zero expectation of finding any clues in that sampling. She studied the truck looking for something sinister, but nothing was obvious to her. They were just about to leave when she noticed the large water jug on the back of the truck. She had seen many outdoor workers carry those jugs as a means of rehydrating while working outdoors and warmer temperatures. They wrapped up their sampling including the jug, gave Mrs. Cheval the keys and again began the return journey to the coroner's office.

On the way, Alicia stopped in the French Quarter so they could grab po'boy sandwiches. Jill had never had one and found it quite delicious. The roll that the sandwich was on was quite different and while she found many of the seafood choices on the menu revolting, she recognized it was the native cuisine of a city on the Gulf Coast. Her chicken club sandwich was warm and tasty and the restaurant was an institution.

Back at the coroner's office they quickly finished their sandwiches and headed back to the lab. Jill walked around checking the analyzers and was delighted to see they all powered up. The two pathologists put together a list of all the specimens they had to process and drew up a plan based on what needed to be shipped out and which specimens would expire if not processed. Jill estimated the processing times of the various tests they would do themselves and then they got to work.

Jill showed Alicia how to run the quality control kits for each machine and an hour after they finished lunch, they were seeing their first results. Chemical panels showed that Mr. Cheval was dehydrated at the time of his death which was not surprising given his reported nausea and vomiting, but like Alicia's earlier testing, they were finding nothing out of the ordinary that a pathologist could conclude would cause death. So they moved on to the surface samples they had taken from the victim's bedroom and truck. One of the analyzers separated chemical compounds using electron microscopy. Mostly they found a variety of farm soils and chemicals. The final sample was from the water reservoir.

"This is weird," Jill said. "Are there evergreen trees grown in Louisiana? Specifically, can you grow a form of nutmeg here?"

"Nutmeg?

"The water in the truck reservoir is contaminated with myristica, which is the Latin name for nutmeg."

"Just for the record, they didn't teach us that in medical school," Alicia said.

Jill laughed and said, "No but I learned a lot of botany as an undergraduate, so I'm pretty good with plants."

"Have you heard of death by nutmeg? Do I need to stay away from eggnog? I love that."

"I haven't heard of death by nutmeg, but then curious teenagers often find new and stupid ways to nearly kill themselves. Remember a couple of years ago, there was a cinnamon challenge where kids would try and swallow a whole teaspoon of cinnamon? It's didn't poison them, but their lungs didn't like it either. I didn't give up cinnamon buns after those reports, so you can continue with the eggnog. Let's contact some poison experts and see if there are any reported toxic effects and what the slow ingestion might lead to. Remember his mother said he would hallucinate more on hot days? Perhaps that's because he was drinking more water from that container."

"I just have an overall question of who and why would someone put nutmeg in a water container. Wouldn't you taste it in the water? Certainly, I taste it in eggnog. Is there a form of nutmeg that isn't so spicy?" Alicia asked.

"We didn't get that far in my botany class for me to answer those questions. We'll have to do some research on it and perhaps we can find the answer. I suspect it is still potent as the scent comes from the leaves and just because the smell has dissipated, it doesn't mean that the leaves' chemicals have changed."

"True, I remember that from our pharmacology class," Alicia

said, then added with a smile, "I'm so glad I called you for help. I feel like we have several avenues to follow up here that might lead us to the real cause and mode of death."

"Let's hope." Jill agreed. "So what else do we have to test? We should find nutmeg in his stomach contents, and in his blood and we'll want to examine his organs to quantify the amount he ingested."

"So besides vomiting and hallucinations, do you remember what else nutmeg intoxication causes? What would have killed him? Cardiac arrhythmia?"

"It would have to be that unless excessive vomiting messed up the electrolytes."

Alicia left the laboratory to walk over to the specimen room where she had stored Mr. Cheval's samples. She could have used his remains for sampling, but the body was decomposing; better to use the preserved tissue and organ samples.

They worked through the afternoon and by the end of the day, Alicia was making a call to the coroner and then to the detectives as they had a murder to investigate.

Detective Scott Briggs and Detective Julie Heyer listened as Alicia explained their findings. Clearly, they'd never had an outside PI and pathologist on the case. Jill described the interview with the mother and their exploration of the work truck. The two detectives had not originally been on the case, so it was all new to them. An hour later they understood that it was indeed a murder. Neither detective had ever investigated a case of murder by poisoning. Detective Heyer had the truck towed to their crime scene yard and they made an appointment with Mrs. Cheval to inform her that her son was murdered. The detectives asked many questions about nutmeg, taking notes, so they could thoroughly explain the case to the victim's mother.

Jill and Alicia worked into the evening to complete the testing they had the equipment for, knowing that any significant findings would have to be officially tested by an accredited lab. Still, the work was interesting for Alicia who hadn't performed such work since her residency. In the back of her mind, she was shaping a proposal to submit to the coroner to get the lab supplied and accredited for future cases. It was a workload she thought she and her fellow pathologists could handle and they could close cases faster and save money in the long run. She found she enjoyed running the analyzers as much as she had weighing organs. The results showed the victim to be dehydrated with other classic signs of someone who'd vomited a lot before his death. The examination of his stomach and intestines showed evidence of nutmeg ingestion. By the end of the day, Jill's work was done and the detectives and Alicia would take it from there. Jill was booked for two additional days in New Orleans as she'd allotted extra time when she booked the trip to spend exploring the city. She now had two days in front of her to check out the museums and atmosphere of the Big Easy, the nickname of the city. Alicia would join her at night when she finished work. Tonight, fresh with the success of identifying a puzzling cause of death, they were celebrating with a fine dinner at a French restaurant.

# CHAPTER 9

*J*ill was on a streetcar the next morning with a
destination of the Café Du Monde. She'd never had
the beignets that were famously served along with
chicory coffee. She was looking forward to both. The café would
place her squarely in the French Quarter which was a good
starting place to start her exploration. Later she planned to catch
the Katrina museum to learn about the devastating hurricane that
hit the city eleven years prior. She'd never lived in an area that
was prone to hurricanes, but unlike the earthquakes in her home
state; hurricanes gave residents up to a week's notice to get out of
harm's way.

She was enjoying her coffee and reading her email. When she
noted an email from Jo. She smiled as she read. Jo was arriving
that evening from Wisconsin for a financial seminar at a hotel
about five blocks away from her current position and remarked
that she had time to do work for Jill after they had dinner if she
needed help.

Jill replied, making plans to meet and introduce her to Alicia.
She provided a summary of Mr. Cheval and noted that the case

was in the hands of the New Orleans police and she was no longer doing any work on it. She then called Nathan.

"Hi sweetie."

"How's the Big Easy? Are you enjoying it and is your case solved?"

"I'm eating beignets and coffee at the Café Du Monde and enjoying the experience. The cause and mode of death has been determined for Alicia's victim, and now there are detectives working the case, so my work is finished."

"Are you sure? Lately, it seems like every case has resulted in you doing the detective work. What about the evil spirits? Did you test for them?" Nathan asked with ample humor in his voice. He'd loved the idea of Jill chasing evil spirits.

"That was really interesting. I now understand a little more about Hoodoo and Voodoo as Caribbean religions. The first set of detectives did sloppy work; when the mom said that her son was killed by evil spirits, if they asked her what she meant, they would have learned she meant someone who has an evil spirit killed him. Quite a distinction. These new detectives seem competent so I don't anticipate having anything more to do with this case. I just got an email from Jo and she's arriving tonight for a conference, so we'll be together without a murder case for once."

"That's great!"

"We're eating at a French restaurant tonight so maybe I can tell you about some great wine later."

"I don't know about that. I think some of the finest wines in the world are produced here in California. If you see a label you like, take a picture for me."

Nathan was a famed wine label designer and created other marketing materials for vineyards and he was always looking for innovative designs.

"Will do. Well, I better get moving, it's going to get humid as the day rolls on and you know how much I hate humidity. Love you, bye."

"Love you too and have fun."

Jill started walking down the various streets of the Quarter, admiring the architecture of the buildings. She noted that she was in a residential area and pulled up the email on Mr. Cheval that Alicia had sent her. She was looking for the address of where the body was found as perhaps it might be nearby. Finding the address and locating it on a map on her phone as two blocks away, she decided to walk over and look.

She was halfway down the block when she noticed police activity farther down the street. Perhaps it was the crime scene team. She arrived to find detectives Briggs and Heyer in an alley watching the crime scene technicians collecting evidence. She could see recognition in their eyes.

"What are you doing on this street Dr. Quint? It's not exactly a tourist destination," Briggs asked.

"Funny you should say that as I was playing tourist; I had breakfast at the Café Du Monde and was exploring the French Quarter and noted I was in a residential area. So I brought up Alicia's notes on the case and noted the address was close by. I couldn't resist coming by to see where Mr. Cheval was found."

Jill found herself being questioned by the detectives as they watched their technicians. Like Alicia, they were interested in some of her stranger cases. When she mentioned her work with the FBI, Interpol, and Police Scotland, she could see they accepted her level of expertise.

"Have you discovered anything useful here? Did he die here or was he dumped here?"

"Dumped or dragged," Heyer replied.

"Any video footage to document how he got here?" Jill asked.

"We're going to knock on doors and find out. He left his friend's car at the end of this street," Briggs said. "I'm guessing he weaved down the street and collapsed not far from here. I think then that someone dragged him into the alley to delay discovery of his body. The patrol officers that were the first responders to this scene found him partially covered by debris and it's not something you do if you're feeling nauseated. You don't lay down and cover yourself with leaves."

"True," Jill said. "Do you have any idea of a motive?"

"None, but then we've only been on the case for a few hours," Heyer said.

"Did you learn anything from Mrs. Cheval?

"Pretty much the same story as you and Alicia relayed to us."

Jill couldn't think of anything more she could add to the scene and so said, "I'm going to continue on my tour of the Quarter. If I can be of any help, don't hesitate to call."

Heyer said, "I don't think the department could afford your consulting fees."

Jill detected sarcasm in the detective's voice and replied with her hands forming quotes in the air, "Actually, my only 'fee' as you say was my plane ticket to get here. Alicia is housing me and my services are free to the Coroner's office. Alicia pleaded poverty and paid me with an intriguing case."

She turned and walked the way she had come to return to the more touristy parts of the Quarter. She heard a conversation behind her, but ignored it and set out for her first of two museums. The Katrina museum was amazing as she learned so much about the hurricane - the erosion of the wetlands and the dikes that failed. It helped that she'd driven through the Ninth Ward and saw the lingering devastation.

She had lunch at a wonderful little Creole restaurant and then took the trolley for a visit to the WWII museum. She didn't know why, but it felt strange that the museum was in New Orleans as it didn't seem like a military town. Perhaps there were a lot of veterans living there or maybe there was a military base nearby. She thought she knew most of the big points of the war, but found she learned many new facts about it. She hadn't studied the war since high school and there were new details about old wars discovered all of the time.

As she was walking toward the exit, her cell phone rang with a New Orleans number. It was probably Alicia calling from an extension at the coroner's office she decided, and offered a friendly, "Hello".

"Hello Dr. Quint, this is Detective Heyer and we've decided to take you up on your offer of free help."

Jill was surprised by the caller and the request, "Okay, what can I do for you?"

"We'd like you to come down to the station to consult with you on our findings so far. If you tell me your location, I'll send a patrol car to give you a ride."

Jill shrugged over the request and said, "I'm at the exit of the WWII Museum. Your patrol car should be able to easily find me here."

There was a slight pause before Heyer asked, "Did you finish your tour? It's a very good museum."

"Yes, I was walking toward the exit when I saw a NOLA number come up on my phone."

"Okay, we'll see you shortly."

Jill tried to do a search on the police department while she was driven to their location. It was a large department for the size of the city and they were living with a consent decree which meant they'd had bad leadership at some time in their past. The building was north of the Superdome, located next to the courts, and was a standard issue government ugly beige building.

Jill found herself in the detective division a short time later. The detectives waved her into a small conference room containing a file and they sat around the table.

Briggs started, "We've been slow to collect evidence and investigate this murder. We'd like to fix that by making use of your services while you're available."

"Did you make any calls and check out my reputation?"

"Of course. We may have been slow to come on to this case,

but we're not stupid. We didn't want to make the case worse than it was already was."

Jill just smiled, impressed with their diligence She would check out the consent decree if she had time later to get a sense of its impact on the transformation of the department.

Briggs opened the file saying, "The poisoning is one of the most unusual murder weapons I've come across in my fifteen years on the job. I understand you have a toxicology background. If you were going to poison someone, would this be your murder weapon of choice?"

"That's a curious question," Jill said thinking about it for a moment, then she replied, "No."

"Why not?" asked Briggs.

Jill thought about what she disliked about the nutmeg and replied, "It's too slow and inexact."

"How so?" asked Heyer.

"Mr. Cheval was poisoned daily Monday thru Friday for perhaps a month. The murder weapon depended on him drinking water from a publicly available tank on the back of his truck. If I were going to kill someone with poison, I'd use a much swifter agent in a far more deserted location like administering a paralyzing agent in Death Valley. My victim's bones would be picked cleaned by animals long before he or she would be discovered."

"Remind us never to anger you," Heyer said with a slight smile at the doctor's gruesome description.

"Yes this agent of death tells you something about the killer. My first thought is a female," Jill said.

"Why," asked Briggs. Jill couldn't decipher whether the detective agreed with her or not.

Jill started to count the reasons, "One, poison deaths are more often female; two, this murder took patience something a female perpetrator is more likely to have, and three, the victim suffered for the past month with nausea and hallucinations and that also speaks to me as female."

Briggs looked at Heyer and Jill and said, "Remind me daily not to make you mad in case I forget. I'd rather just take a bullet than suffer for weeks thank you."

"Exactly," Jill said with a smile, "Guys more often think of murder as a task to be done, a box to be checked. We women want you to suffer for your alleged offenses and we want to escape prosecution. So kill slowly and quietly."

"You're scaring me Dr. Quint."

"Hey, you're a gun-toting detective who has arrested his share of scary and psychotic people over the course of your career, I don't believe you," Jill replied with a grin.

With a smile, Heyer moved on to the folder.

"The crime scene techs are taking apart the work truck. We debated fingerprinting it and in the end we just printed the water reservoir, there were too many prints otherwise."

"You might want to print the left and right side of the truck as well about four inches from the reservoir out. I'm a short female and I had to brace my hand on the side of the truck while I stretched to see where the top opening was, assuming our perpetrator is a short female."

Heyer wrote that in their notes while Briggs texted something.

"Have you located a nutmeg expert?" Jill asked.

"Is there such a thing?" Heyer asked.

"I'm sure there is perhaps in the Caribbean or Indonesia where the plant is grown. There might be a botanical expert somewhere in the United States."

"Why do we need an expert?" Briggs asked though Jill could see he had reasons of his own and was just curious about her opinion.

"Both Alicia and I were curious about the lack of nutmeg taste in the water. You know how strong nutmeg is for say french toast or eggnog. To be in concentration strong enough to poison, the water container should have smelled like eggnog, but it didn't to me. So beyond the knowledge of how to use it for poison, your perp needed to know how to get the scent out of it. I don't know enough about this botanical plant to know if it changes chemical composition as the scent changes, but I would call the botany department at one of your local universities as a starting point to answer that question."

"Are we looking for a nutmeg expert there?" Heyer asked.

"I doubt if you would find one. The plant is a part of the ever-green family and I'd bet the university has an expert for that plant species," Jill said and then a thought occurred to her. "If you would like, I could run down that clue for you. There's a university near my home – the University of California, Davis, that has a large botany department. I could speak to those experts about this question or any others you have."

"Is there a cost to using their expertise?" Briggs asked.

"I wouldn't think so unless you need the person for court testimony. I'm an alumnus of the department in addition to my professional standing in the state and I'm pretty sure I can get your answers for free."

"I think it's unlikely that we would need this expert for court testimony as we likely have other evidence that would connect our perp. We can cross the bridge when we get to it. Call your expert Dr. Quint."

It took Jill awhile to bounce through the school directory to find the expert she needed. Then she had another hour to wait until that person would be available by phone.

In the interim, she returned to the case file and asked, "What are your thoughts on a motive?"

"One of the usual reasons – greed, unrequited love, or jealousy. I don't see overwhelming anger here as the murder took too long to be completed. Anyone powered by a murderous rage would be unlikely to sustain it for this four to six-week poisoning effort," Briggs remarked.

"I would look at jealousy or greed as I haven't come across

unrequited love very often in my cases. What does his social media reveal and have you had time to look at his finances?"

"We haven't got that far in the case – we've barely had time to move beyond the crime scene. I don't even know where nutmeg comes from beyond the spice aisle at my local grocery store," Heyer said.

"When I take on cases officially, I bring a team of experts with me. One is expert at finding finance problems in people and organizations. She happens to be arriving in town this evening and will give us a few hours of 'free' time to scratch the surface of his financial picture as well as those immediate family members, girlfriends, and employers. I have another team member that's a social media maven. She finds all kinds of interesting information on people on Facebook, Instagram, Twitter, basically wherever someone has posted. She is not in town, but I'll see if she has time to donate a few hours of her service. My final team member is an expert interviewer; in the kindest method imaginable, she'll have granny confessing to stealing a stick of gum forty years ago. She'll not be able to assist as she's not on the scene. I leave town in a day and a half, so this is just an outline of the resources you'll have for say the next thirty-six hours."

"Dr. Quint, as an expert you know that it is improbable that we will solve this case in that time frame," Briggs said.

"I know. I was just giving you some details beyond the questions of nutmeg of how I can help. If you like I'll sign a confidentiality agreement so you can give me access to the victim's personal information – name, address, date of birth, social security number, etc. I need that information to start collecting information beyond the poison involved in this case. That's if you want my help in other areas."

The two detectives looked at each other wordlessly communicating as partners sometimes can, then Heyer said, "Let us run that by our Lieutenant and with his approval, I'll be back with a form to have you sign."

The two detectives exited the room while Jill settled back for the call from California on the plant biology of nutmeg. She hoped the professor she'd tracked down would have her answers or could connect her to someone that did.

Minutes later her phone rang with a call origin of Davis, California showing on her screen. It must be her expert.

"Hello, this is Dr. Jill Quint."

"Hi, this is Ann Watson, professor of plant botany. I received a message I was supposed to call you Dr. Quint. What can I do for you?"

"I have a B.S. from Davis in botany conferred many years ago. I'm also a forensic pathologist and I'm assisting the New Orleans police with a murder case. The victim was poisoned by nutmeg."

"Nutmeg? Wow, that's unusual. I don't think I've ever seen that used in a TV law and order episode. How does it kill?"

"It causes hallucinations, vomiting, and eventual heart arrhythmia if you get enough of the acid in the fruit. The plant is a member of the evergreen family and I understand that's your area of expertise."

"I'm the faculty expert on evergreens, yes, but I know next to nothing about nutmeg as it's not a common evergreen under study by this university. Ask me about coastal redwoods or giant sequoias."

"I may ask for a recommendation for another expert, but perhaps you can answer a question for me. The nutmeg that was used to kill our victim was put in one of those standard water jugs you see on the backs of utility trucks that outdoor workers use to stay hydrated. However, the water didn't have an odor of nutmeg. So my botany question is, do plants or evergreens change chemical composition as they lose their flavoring? We're trying to figure out how you poison someone with nutmeg in drinking water without the victim tasting it."

"That's a great question. I have a few grad students that I'll be meeting with later today. Can we research your question and get back to you? We might be able to do a few lab experiments to verify how you would create tasteless nutmeg as I think they sell the whole nutmeg in the spice aisle at our local store. That's the heart of your question, yes?"

"Yes, exactly. How does a plant retain its identity to still be called nutmeg without having any flavor to it."

"I'll get back to you and I thank you for asking the most interesting question of my week and really month; I love a good challenge."

The two women ended their call having made follow-up arrangements for the answer to Jill's intriguing question.

# CHAPTER 10

The two detectives returned to the conference room with a sheet of paper for Jill to sign on confidentiality. After she signed it, they discussed how they would handle Jo having access to Mr. Cheval's personal data. Then they tossed out motive ideas but really it was too early in the case to zero in on it. The detectives would interview the victim's son and his mother to see if they could learn anything from the two of them. Of course, the child's mother would be the prime suspect, but for some reason Jill wasn't thinking it was her. The two parents had never lived together and seemed to be sharing their child well based on what the grandmother said. There seemed to be neither the passion nor the sophistication required for this murder. The perpetrator needed to know that nutmeg could be used as a poison, how to use it, and how to make it tasteless.

"My plant expert is supposed to call me back on the nutmeg taste question. They may buy nutmeg from their local grocery store and do some experiments on it, but at least we've got experts working on the question of how the poison was created. This is a sophisticated murder scenario and I doubt that it's a family member," Jill said.

"It's the first place we'll look especially given the victim's mother and child's mother are the closest relatives to the victim and poison is usually a female's choice of murder weapon, but I hear what you're saying about the sophistication of this murder," Briggs said.

"What about his job or his hobbies? What do we know about that? His mother didn't mention any hobbies to me as it seemed his calendar was full of work and caring for his son. I believe his job was that of an agriculture inspector," Jill said.

"It's on our list to explore. As he was a state employee, there's a job description on the state's website, but we'll need to speak to his supervisor and co-workers as routine detective work," Heyer noted.

"It's an interesting connection – an agriculture specialist and a death by poison from a plant," Jill said. "I think I'll spend some time looking at that connection, and with my botany degree it's an area I have some expertise in. When you interview the co-workers, I'd love to be there. Are you doing that today?"

"We have to as tomorrow's Saturday and we're not likely to find the people we need at the job site. In fact, we probably should head there now as we have at least an hour drive to Baton Rouge and we need to notify our fellow departments that we're stepping into their territory. Give us fifteen minutes to make arrangements and then you can join us," Heyer said.

On schedule, Jill found herself in the back of a patrol unit on Interstate 10 heading northwest. When she lived in Los Angeles, she'd been on this same Interstate just two-thousand miles to the west. The road was in better shape with less traffic than the version she'd driven in southern California. Soon they were out of New Orleans and close to agriculture fields.

"What kinds of crops does the state grow?"

"Ah, I don't know," replied Heyer. "None of my family is into farming and we've never had to know the answer to that question as a part of a crime scene investigation."

Jill used her cellphone to look up the question.

"Hmm, your state website says it's sugar cane. That's followed by rice, soybeans, cotton, and corn for grain," looking out the window at the passing crops. Reading further she noted that a farm they passed was likely growing sugarcane based on the preparation of the ground and current planting. It was planting time for sugarcane. She wondered what crops her victim had specialized in and hoped they would pass a cotton plant as she'd never seen it growing. Soon the farms were ending and they were arriving on the edge of Baton Rouge. With GPS providing directions they soon arrived at Mr. Cheval's office building.

From the front seat Detective Briggs said, "We're meeting his supervisor, Aimee Fontaine, and I expect she'll direct us to his coworkers and friends at work. Hopefully, they're in the office or we might end up making some house calls. We may be later than expected getting you back to the city."

Jill nodded as she exited the car, and added, "Feel free to introduce me as Dr. Jill Quint, a forensic pathologist. Ms. Fontaine doesn't have to know that I'm not your local coroner."

"Sounds like a plan, we'd rather not be distracted by explaining your role in this investigation."

A short time later they were shown into a conference room by Aimee Fontaine. As they entered, Detective Heyer requested, "Before we get too involved in our conversation we would appreciate you requesting any staff that you would consider co-workers or friends of Mr. Cheval to stay here so we can interview them. It will save us and them the trouble of being disturbed at home."

Ms. Fontaine left the room to make the employee notifications and returned saying, "I made contact with all but Keith who is off today but lives in New Orleans. He took the day off to do something at his child's school so you should be able to find him later."

The detectives noted his contact information and moved on to begin questioning Ms. Fontaine after stating that Mr. Cheval was a victim of murder.

"Were you aware that Mr. Cheval wasn't feeling well over the last month?" Detective Briggs asked.

"Yes as he took time off to see a few doctors for severe nausea. I think he may have called in sick one day as well. The last time I spoke with him, the doctors hadn't been able to determine the cause of his nausea."

"Do you know who fills the water jugs carried on your state trucks?" Jill asked.

Ms. Fontaine looked sick when she realized why Jill asked the question. She said is a voice that had lost its power, "Do you mean to say he was made ill by the water jug? We have a department procedure that calls for the driver to fill their own jug as well as to empty it at the end of the shift and leave the cap off overnight, so mold or other agents don't grow in the water. Did mold kill him?"

"No," replied Detective Heyer. "You seem to know that particular policy well."

"I've been in a supervisor position for just over six months. Before that I did the same job Julien did including filling my own water jug. We weren't assigned the same vehicle every day – we have more staff than cars so employees vary their days in the office and in the field so that the cars are always utilized."

"Has any other employee reported being nauseated?" Jill asked.

Ms. Fontaine thought for a few moments, then shook her head, "No, none of my employees have experienced what Julien did. I've had a few absences related to colds mostly in parents of young children and I have an employee who's going through chemo at the moment and doesn't feel good some days due to that."

"Can we have a copy of your water jug policy," asked Heyer.

"Sure," replied Aimee. "Does that mean that whatever killed Julien was in the water jug on his truck?"

"Yes you could assume that ma'am," replied Briggs.

"Oh! Was it a quick acting poisoning then?"

"How did you arrive at that conclusion?"

The supervisor paused, worrying about the suspicion in the detective's voice, and said with a question in her voice, "Because no one else among my staff is dead."

There was a silence in the room as the detectives waited for Ms. Fontaine to add more and so she did.

"I don't understand how that could happen as we each fill our own jug and Julien wouldn't have poisoned himself. He had too much to live for and was a contented man. Someone would have had to follow his truck each day and add whatever poison to the jug when he was out of eyesight of the truck. Typically we stop by farm fields and take samples and so the truck is in view of the driver. The only time it wouldn't be in view was if he came back to the office before going back out or if he stopped for a food or bathroom break," Aimee said and then added, "Whomever murdered him would have to be in our parking lot at the beginning of the shift to figure out which truck he drove and which fields he was visiting. His area was too large for someone to hope that they might spot him during the workday."

The detectives took notes during her final explanation. It was a complicated setup and again spoke to the sophistication of the perpetrator in this murder.

"You have cameras atop this building monitoring the parking lot?" Jill asked.

"No, we haven't had any crime or vandalism on the site and we don't do anything secretive here. We're resources to the state's farmers. We're experts in things like bugs, plants, herbicides, pesticides, fertilizers, seeds, and crop production. Occasionally we do weights and measures. The only time we make a farmer angry is when we come across an illegal pesticide that they're using which is a rare event."

Jill considered herself an expert in pesticides. She knew and understood the chemical compounds of the most popular pesticides used in America. She was committed to creating organic pesticides for use in her vineyard and so far she had been successful.

"What kind of illegal pesticides do you find around the state? And if you find them, what are the consequences for the farmer?" Jill asked.

"It's not so much that we find illegal herbicides and pesticides used rather they are applied to crops that they don't work on or they are applied in a way that is harmful to another farmer's crop's health. The best example of that is Dicamba. If a farmer is not careful when they apply that pesticide then the wind will carry it and damage nearby crops that it's not supposed to be used on. Also, it should not be used on cotton and soybeans, two of our most important crops in Louisiana. Some states have gone so far as to ban Dicamba, but so far we haven't had enough farmer complaints to go that far."

Jill had heard of Dicamba as it was considered deadly to vineyard crops. She also knew that the state of California had recently labeled it as cancer-causing. In her mind, the passions surrounding Dicamba were between Monsanto and the states. Individual farmers either loved it because it helped them control weeds, or they hated it because they had lost crops from the drift of Dicamba during the application process.

"What's been the state's role in mediating the use of Dicamba among farmers?" Jill asked.

"It's been around for nearly fifty years and we average a few fights a year between farmers with allegations of damage to crops from Dicamba. Typically our inspectors will take a plant sample and send it to the lab to be tested for Dicamba. If we have a positive, we have issued notices of warnings, suspended applicators' certifications, and assessed fines and penalties totaling hundreds of thousands of dollars. That usually gets the farmer's attention, as they don't have much margin on the profit they make growing crops."

"Are you aware if Julian Cheval collected any samples that became problematic for the farmers?" Briggs asked.

"Off the top of my head, no. I'll need to review his records to see what he was in the middle of."

"Is it something we could review," Jill asked. "I have a degree in botany, so I'll understand a lot of your nomenclature."

Aimee frowned and asked, "I'm confused - aren't you a pathologist? Don't you look at the dead?"

Jill smiled and thought I do more than look at the dead, but said instead, "The autopsy is completed and now I'm using my botany background to assist the detectives in solving this crime. May I look at his records?" she asked again.

Aimee Fontaine thought for a moment about privacy rights of the work they did and decided she wanted to do what she could to help find Julien's killer. She'd asked for forgiveness later for any rules violations she did in connection with letting the officers look at the office activity of Julien.

"Do you have time now? I can show you his desk."

They looked at their watches calculating hours left in the day. Briggs said to Heyer, "You go with Dr. Quint and I'll begin interviewing his coworkers. I expect you to be done sooner than I so contact me if you can help me with the interviews." She nodded and they all stood up to exit the small conference room.

imee showed Jill and the detective Julien's workspace. She also brought up on the screen the computer system the inspectors used to document their activities in the field. She would really have to ask forgiveness from the department head of Agriculture and Forestry. She knew she shouldn't be sharing the software program without a search warrant, but again she wanted to help. She'd met Julian's son, Jayden, and she thought it was terrible that he was now fatherless.

After a quick search of the desk yielded mostly office supplies with a few notes of things to follow up on, the two women turned to the computer hoping the answers were there. Jill started running down each entry in the spreadsheet that related to the activities that Julien performed in his work as an agriculture inspector. Jill studied the column titles and then moved down the page to make sure she understood the issues and terms. Fresh in the back of her head was the discussion they'd had with Ms. Fontaine concerning the herbicide. Jill noted that one of the last entries into the spreadsheet that Julien had made was related to Dicamba. How curious.

They finished going through any possible clue in Julian's

office. Jill had saved a copy of the spreadsheet on a zip drive, and also emailed it to herself and they joined Detective Briggs for the interviews. He was just finishing up the last interview and so they exited the building together. The coworkers had not been much help and it was the detective's sense that they just weren't close. Several of them mentioned the individual that they would stop and interview on their return to New Orleans. It seemed that the issue was geography. These co-workers lived in Baton Rouge while Julien lived in New Orleans and the cities were too far apart for much socializing to take place. The other co-worker lived in Bywater which was close to Julien's ninth ward home. So they occasionally would meet outside of work and to commute together a couple of times a month. The detective hadn't found any helpful information from his interviews. They piled into the patrol car and headed back south to New Orleans. Again Jill observed crops from the window and thought about farming and the hazards of picking a wrong herbicide or pesticide.

They would interview a Mr. Keith Townsend in about fifty minutes and then they would be done for the day. Jill planned to look at the spreadsheet and explore any issues listed there. She hadn't noticed any financial fines or crop destruction as a resolution to problems Julien might have encountered in his farm surveys. Finally, they turned down the street where Mr. Townsend lived. Jill hadn't been in this part of New Orleans and like the French Quarter, Garden District, and Ninth Ward, Bywater had a unique look to it. There were lots of murals painted on walls and the predominate architecture style was the shotgun style – long narrow houses.

They parked in front of a house and got out to walk to the front door. Just as they reached the front stoop, the door opened and a man in his 30s stepped out and onto the stoop.

"Hi I'm Keith Townsend. You must be the detectives from the New Orleans Police Department. I have young children inside and my wife just arrived home to corral them. Since this discussion is about my murdered coworker I prefer to have it outside, away from the young ears of my children."

"I understand Mr. Townsend," said Detective Heyer. "Is there someplace we could go and sit down to talk? Perhaps there's a park nearby?"

"Actually we could just go in my backyard, the children won't be able to hear me outside."

They followed him through a side gate into a small backyard that had a picnic table that they could all sit at for their discussion. Once seated, Detective Briggs began the interview.

"We just came from talking to your co-workers and Ms. Fontaine at your office. Sorry to intrude into your home, but you're a vital part of this investigation. From all accounts, you were the co-worker closest to Julien Cheval."

"I would agree with that," Keith said. "I hung out with Julien as we were the two employees that lived in New Orleans and we carpooled to work at least once a week. You get to know someone when you're stuck commuting. He was a good man and father."

"How long have you known Julien?"

"We've worked together perhaps seven years. He knows my wife and kids and I know his mom and son. I don't think I ever met the mother of his son in part because they were never married or lived together. We held the same position for the state but had different geographic responsibilities. What else can I tell you?"

"You knew he wasn't feeling well the last several weeks?" Heyer asked.

"Yes, you could see that he lost weight, and I encountered him in the bathroom throwing up at least twice. On his last day of work, he asked if I could drive him as he wasn't feeling well. So I picked him up but as we traveled through the French Quarter, he asked me to pull over so he wouldn't vomit in my car. As he didn't want me to be late to work, he said not to wait for him and he'd call his mom to pick him up and take him home. I knew his nausea was bad, but I never would have left him if I thought it was bad enough to kill him."

This last statement was made with several large swallows by Keith who seemed to need time to gather himself before he continued.

Detective Heyer waited a few moments then asked her next question, "Was he worried about anything in his private life or at the office? Had anything unusual happened in say the last four to six weeks?"

"You think he was killed because of something at the office?"

"We have no evidence that leads us to think that, but at this stage of the investigation we've not yet found any motive for Julien Cheval's murder."

"You haven't? It's been several days since he died. Why don't you have any suspects yet?"

"Well for one thing in real life we don't solve murder investigations as quickly as they do on television shows, and my second comment is that it wasn't identified as a murder until late yesterday."

"Are you kidding? Why would a young otherwise healthy man die on the street in New Orleans? It wasn't cold, he wasn't drunk, and he had no diseases that would have killed him. Why wasn't his death suspicious from the beginning?"

"We'll explain that later to you," Briggs said. "Let's get back to the detective's question. Was Mr. Cheval worried about anything? Had anything unusual happened at home or at work that you were aware of?"

Keith glanced out into space thinking about the interactions he had with Julian over the time frame specified by the detectives. Then he remembered the monster truck interaction that Julien had described. It was the only thing he could think was unusual in their daily lives.

"You're going to think this is weird, but Julian had an interaction in a field with a monster truck about a month ago."

"Tell us more about the interaction," Heyer said. "What's a monster truck and how did the interaction feel strange to Julien?"

"Julien was passing by a field somewhere between New Orleans and Baton Rouge and noticed a field that wasn't looking healthy around the edges. So he parked his vehicle and took a sample of one of the plants to test for Dicamba. Unfortunately we lose a fair amount of healthy crops to the drift from other farmers spraying their fields with the herbicide. Usually we take a sample of the plant to verify the presence of the herbicide and then we issue penalties or other corrective actions to the farmer who uses the substance. This also gives the farmer with damage to their crops evidence to collect reimbursement from the farmer who damaged his or her crops."

"Do you do a lot of sort of refereeing between farmers?" Jill asked.

Keith thought for a moment and then replied, "I suppose so in any given season it can be from ten to twenty-five percent of the findings in my role as an agricultural supervisor."

"So what is a monster truck and what's its role in this story?" asked Heyer.

"Oh yeah, the monster truck. It really shook up Julien. As he was bending down to snip a sample, he saw dust in the distance like you see when a truck travels on a dirt road. The cloud of dust continued his way and he could hear the roar of an engine. It really freaked him out because once the cloud of dust cleared, there was a large pickup truck with enormous tires and two men inside the cab and another two seated on chairs mounted in the truck bed. They were seated behind rifles and at first Julian thought he was going to die. One of the men in the back of the truck bed pulled something from his side and Julien thought it was a pistol. However, it turned out to be a cell phone and the guy took his picture. Then the truck spun a one-hundred-eighty degree turn and took off towards wherever it came from blowing more dust at him."

"Did he report this once he got back to the office? Is this how you heard about it?"

"No, it was such a bizarre occurrence that Julien felt he might be laughed at or told that he was dreaming as none of us have ever encountered a monster truck let alone what was mounted in the back of it. So we went to lunch that day and he told me about it."

"And even after telling you at lunch he never reported it to Ms. Fontaine?" Briggs asked.

"Not that I know of."

"Do you remember what day this was?" Jill asked.

"No it was sometime a month ago, or so."

"Did you pay for your lunch with the debit or credit card that might contain the date of the monster truck sighting?" Heyer asked.

"That's a good question, let me pull out my bank app and I'll look and see. I often do use my debit card."

Silence reigned while he hit several buttons on his smartphone. Moments later he looked up and said, "It happened on October second."

With the date in mind, Jill opened the file she'd sent to herself from Julien's office. She found the specimen that he submitted on that date. Actually there were two specimens so he must've gone to another field on that day. She debated sharing the information with Keith but decided she didn't want to snitch on Ms. Fontaine's release of the information.

"Do you have an address of where this encounter occurred?" Heyer asked.

"No, but I believe he submitted a sample to the lab and there's part of that paperwork where we indicate the geographical coordinates of where we collected the sample so I'm sure the supervisor can give you the address."

Heyer looked at Jill who nodded.

"Did Julian connect his illness to the encounter with the monster truck?" Jill asked

"If he did, he didn't tell me. I know at one point he thought he had the flu, then he worried about bigger things like cancer causing his nausea but so far the doctors hadn't found anything seriously wrong with Julian. I remember the day that it happened I offered to go collect a specimen for him but he said it was such a scary encounter that he wouldn't do that to me as a friend."

"Did you ever hear what the results of the tests were from that field?" Jill asked.

"No, but ordinarily it wouldn't come up in the conversation. We each did our work and when we met for lunch or carpooling or just after work we didn't talk about work we talked the Saints or our families."

"One more question Keith, when you left the parking lot at your office to go collect samples in the field what was your process? Did you have a vehicle assigned to you? Did you have to fill the truck with supplies that you needed for collections, did you fill it up with gas, or fill up the water jug on the truck? What did you do to make it easy for you to do your work in the field?" Jill asked.

Keith gave her a look that suggested that he found her question unconnected to the murder of his friend and co-worker but he complied with her question.

"Ms. Fontaine probably told you that we don't have vehicles assigned to each of us personally. So I would go see her assistant as she kept the key box for all the vehicles. She would give me the keys and I would go out to the truck and take a look at what supplies were already stocked. Sometimes I didn't need anything. At other times the supplies were really low. If it needed gas I have a gas card assigned through the office. As for the water jug; we have a good department procedure for keeping it clean, but I never trusted that and I always brought my own bottle of water or soda. Does that answer your question?"

"Yes thank you," Jill said as she looked at the two detectives indicating she had no further questions.

"Did Julien Cheval ever indicate that he was having problems with his child's mother?" Detective Heyer asked.

"No ma'am, that part of his life seemed to flow smoothly. If he wanted extra time with Jayden she would give it to him. If he needed to switch weekends, she was flexible. They seem to be more friends than former lovers."

"Mr. Townsend, we appreciate you taking the time to talk to us today about Julian Cheval. How should we contact you if other questions arise?" asked Detectives Briggs.

"You can contact me at the cell phone number that Ms. Fontaine gave you to arrange this meeting."

The detectives asked where Jill wanted to be dropped off and the car headed in that direction.

"What do you think about the monster truck story?" Heyer asked Jill.

"I know this is going to sound weird, but I likely had the same experience maybe twenty years ago on the island of Maui in Hawaii. A friend and I were in a rental car in the north part of the island which was pretty deserted. There was no reason for tourists to head down the road other than to see what was there and so we did. The paved road ended and we could see a dirt path ahead and so we decided to turn around as our curiosity had been sated and we didn't want to damage a rental car. As I was making the three-point turn, a monster truck just as described by Mr. Townsend came out a grove of pineapple plants. It was filled with native Hawaiians giving us the stink eye. To this day, I don't know if I got the stink eye for being a Caucasian on land owned by native Hawaiians for centuries, or perhaps they were protecting a crop that I wasn't supposed to see like marijuana or poppies that might be produced into heroin. At the time I remember thinking that it was overkill - the big tough guys, the monster truck and if only they put a sign up a few hundred feet back that said 'private property' we would never have gone down the road."

"That's an interesting story," Detective Heyer commented. "We have some of that in Louisiana. We have arrests for growing mari-juana, but I can't recall any arrest for opium poppies or coca leaves. I assumed you were able to note the geographic coordinates of the two samples he took on October second. We could go there first thing in the morning and check the fields out."

"Also let's check in with Ms. Fontaine to find out what happened to the sample. Maybe that will tell us something about the case," suggested Jill.

The detectives let her off at Alicia's house and when she entered she found her home from work.

"Hey how did your day of sightseeing go?"

"It was different. I started in the French Quarter at Café Du Monde. Later because I was close by I checked the location where your dead body came from. I spoke with detectives Briggs and Heyer and offered my services for free as long as I'm staying with you. I was just finishing up at the WWII museum when I got the call that they were interested in including me on the case. So then I spent the afternoon in Baton Rouge and then back in an area called Bywater and then the detectives dropped me off at your house. Tonight we're having dinner with my good friend Jo since she's in town for a convention. I think I mentioned she's my financial expert on some of these cases."

"Wow, I had a boring day compared to you! I didn't actually have any autopsies today so I finished up with paperwork for prior cases including some test results."

"Look at the bright side, it's good news that no one died in a manner in this region that required your services as a forensic pathologist!"

"There is that! Have you found a motive yet for the murder of Mr. Cheval?"

"No we have some clues to follow up on and the police have yet to interview the mother of Julian's son, but my bet early on is it has something to do with his work."

"His work? What's so dangerous about being an agricultural inspector or whatever his title was I know it was something in agriculture."

"Normally that wouldn't be dangerous, but this is a very unique mode of death and someone with an agriculture background would most likely have the knowledge of how to make nutmeg poisonous. I made a call to my old Alma Mater to speak with a professor whose expertise is evergreens and she has a group of students exploring taking the smell and taste out of nutmeg and then testing the resulting chemical composition to see if it's poison. She said it was the most interesting question she had this month if not for a longer period of time."

"Wow what an exciting day. I can see why you like your current occupation. You get to follow your curiosity all day long and you come across some interesting stuff doing so."

"I do enjoy the investigative side and that was something that we as coroners never get to do, but it feels like a more complete way of serving the dead. Last year I got my private investigators license just to add legitimacy to my work."

"You know if someday you need a second forensic pathologist to join your team full time or even on a casual basis as you seem to do with your teammates, please give me a call and I'll see if I can get away from whatever I'm doing here. I think I would be a better coroner for a variety of reasons if I spent more time with you and your cases."

"I do the occasional open and shut autopsy. In fact, it's more than occasional. I actually agree with the medical examiner about seventy percent of the time so figure that into your desire to work with me - likely about seventy percent of the cases are exactly what you're doing every day on the job here in New Orleans."

"I guess that's a good news, bad news statement. The bad news is not all of your work is exciting, but the good news is there are a lot of good medical examiners out there."

"Exactly. The other issue is you have to be very flexible as I've had cases across the United States as well as in Belgium and the United Kingdom. So that's forced me to learn to work with a variety of law enforcement agencies and understand international laws and customs in regards to autopsies."

"You mean you got to solve cases internationally? Okay! Now I don't care if some of them are boring autopsies, I'd love to try doing one in a foreign country."

Jill just laughed at her statement and said, "Really the job isn't as exotic as it sounds. Now we better go change and get ready to meet one of my teammates for dinner. You'll like her."

"Thanks for the offer, and after a boring paperwork day, I'm looking forward to some girl time and adult conversation."

Jill's eyes crinkled at the thought of sitting for long periods and offered encouragement, "I remember those horrible days."

Jill entered Alicia's spare bedroom and freshened her clothes and makeup and they were back out the door heading for the streetcar stop. She was better at public transportation than Jo, so it made sense for her to head to Jo's hotel then the three of them would walk from there into the French Quarter for dinner. Thirty minutes later, they were seated in a restaurant famous for its courtyard and often live jazz music. Jo was always much more adventurous than Jill in her menu selections, and so they started with grilled alligator as an appetizer while Jo moved on to catfish cooked Creole style, Alicia ordered a Cajun chicken dish, and Jill ordered trout.

After catching up on each other's lives and families the three women moved on to the case at hand. After dinner they planned to move on to a few different bars to try unique New Orleans alcoholic concoctions. Jill and Jo brought tablet computers so they could research and drink at the same time. Alicia was wide-eyed watching them conduct their investigation.

The first bar they tried was close to the restaurant and Jill went through the classic hurricane drink. It was green and sweet with the alcohol well hidden.

"This sort of reminds me of our case in Scotland where much of our research occurred while we were all trying to like scotch whiskey," Jo said. "We solved the case, but only Angela learned to like that spirit. But as spirits go, I must say I like rum-based drinks more, though to be fair to Scotland, here we're not drinking the spirit straight up."

"I think I still would've disliked the scotch if we mixed it with whatever fruit punch is in this hurricane. Still we did try pretty hard to like scotch. Between the visits to the distilleries and the varieties we tasted in that country, I guess we tried ten different scotch whiskeys before we gave it up."

Alicia added, "Bourbon is popular in the South and so I did like you ladies and seriously chased it for a few months trying to find a distillery I liked, but it was a lost cause."

Finished with reminiscing about their time in distilleries they moved on to Jill's case in New Orleans. She brought Jo up to speed on the findings from today's interview.

"The only place I've ever seen monster trucks is at a rally in Green Bay. They made a lot of noise as they crawled over smashed up vehicles like they were toy cars. I have to say that the first three or four passes by the trucks were interesting and then it was boring."

Jill described her encounter with the monster truck while on vacation in Hawaii.

"Trust you to find evil lurking even in paradise. So you think this might be related to illicit marijuana growing? Doesn't that seem a little extreme; to murder someone who didn't even discover your illegal crop?"

"Of course, but then I always think murder is an extreme reaction yet it happens all the time."

"True so what do you want me to research?" Jo asked.

"Well the victim, his mother, and the mother of his son, but I think that will be quick and you'll find nothing unusual there," Jill said passing a piece of paper to Jo with the names and birth dates of the individuals.

"Okay, what else?" Jo asked as she got to work on her three names.

"I don't have names yet, just geographical coordinates, so I need to spend some time doing research on properties to give you additional names."

Soon there was the sound of ambient noise of the bar and Jo's clicks of the keyboard's keys. She'd always been a hard hitting typist and you could hear her typing from another room. Alicia couldn't contribute and so instead watched what they did to investigate someone.

Fifteen minutes later, Jo sat back and said, "You're right there's nothing there other than the evidence of the tragedy of Hurricane Katrina. I can see the transfer of assets as people died during that storm, the gap in employment, the housing repairs, and the ongoing recovery. There's nothing unusual or unexpected financially in their backgrounds. Should we move on to a new bar before our next round of research?"

"Yeah, I'm ready for a new drink and I need your help sorting through corporations. Let's head for the carousel bar which is supposed to make us feel like we are on a carousel."

"Ladies, I'm going to have to leave you here as I have to get up early for a meeting tomorrow. It was a pleasure meeting you Jo," Alicia said and she parted for the streetcar stop.

Two blocks later Jill and Jo turned into the hotel containing the unusual bar and took a seat at the bar. The bar and bar stools rotated around a core area where the bartenders worked. They made a complete revolution every twelve minutes.

"This is unique and I'm glad it's not revolving faster or I might be tossing my drinks," Jill said.

"Yeah you do get sick to your stomach easily, but this is so slow that you'll be okay. Okay, what help do you need with corporations?"

Jill had explained about the victim's encounter with the monster truck and the plant samples.

"So I have the geographic coordinates of the farm, but really, it could be any of nearly a dozen farms close by. Some are easy to figure out the owners and others seem to be corporations. Here are three corporations; can you figure out who the real owner is behind the name?"

"I'll try. Some of these corporations are set up offshore and they're not required to have the same reporting that corporations have in the United States so I may not actually figure out who owns these properties."

"I can imagine that your average soybean farmer couldn't afford an attorney to set up a sophisticated corporation to hide their assets offshore. If that's the conclusion you arrive at then I'll have to figure out some other way to get information on the property. I've been experimenting at home with the drone to get an aerial view of my vineyard. I might be able to get that same look at these properties."

"Did you bring your drone with you?"

"No, but I bet Nathan could overnight it to me. Let me call him right now."

Jill debated calling him from the bar as it was noisy inside, but she put her earbuds on and dialed his number.

"Hey love, how is New Orleans?"

"Fabulous, the food and drinks are awesome and take a look at this bar," she said moving her phone around the bar so Nathan could see its details. "I'm enjoying this fun bar with Jo and we're looking up some information on a farmer, actually a group of farmers between New Orleans and Baton Rouge. If I could get an aerial view of the area it might help me figure out the right piece of property. Would you mind getting my drone from my house and overnighting it to me?"

"How about if I do you one better. I signed a contract with a distillery in Louisiana. I'm leaving in a few hours from San Francisco and I land in your neck of the woods around nine tomorrow morning."

"Yeah! I'm excited you're coming and I'll extend my stay here. I didn't know that you were under consideration for a client here. Congratulations on getting the new client! Maybe Jo will have a chance to have dinner with us one of the nights we're all here."

They spoke for a while longer and Nathan gave Jill his hotel name and address so she could move from Alicia's house to the hotel tomorrow. She hoped the New Orleans police would be glad to have her assistance for a while longer.

Jill said to Jo, "Nathan will be here early tomorrow morning and he's bringing my drone with him so that will allow me to look at the various plots of land from the sky. The silly man never tells me about potential new clients because some of them turn him down. I wouldn't care if he failed to get a contract with a new customer. I know he does great work, and that's all that matters. Did you make any progress on identifying who the owners are on these various land titles?"

"Gee whiz Jill! I've had the names for all of five minutes that's too little time to make progress on your question," Jo said and paused as Jill looked at her expectantly, "but I'm good at this and I did get you two of the three names."

Jill leaned in to give her a fist bump, "Yeah, I knew you would be fast at this! Do the names tell you anything?"

"Yes and no. In the brief look at the ownership structure the corporations were created because these are family farmers. I haven't gotten far looking up these families, but two of them date back nearly one-hundred years. I think there are two ways to look at that information - these corporations are too old to have anything hinky going on, or these are old family operated businesses and they have a lot to lose if anything is discovered about them."

"Those are good observations," Jill said looking over at Jo's drink. "Should we head over to a new bar as it appears we finished our drinks here?"

"The next bar will be my last. I won't function well at the conference tomorrow if I keep imbibing these delightful southern concoctions."

"I know what you mean, if I have one drink more I might be drunk flying my drone tomorrow morning and that's a sure way to get into trouble," Jill said with a laugh. "You have any requests for what our final bar should be?"

"You know me I'm easy. You've done a good job picking our bars so far this evening, so you pick the final one."

"Okay, how about if we go by the Café Du Monde and get some beignets to go and then we'll settle in at an outdoor bar across from the French Market? From there we can walk the riverfront back to your hotel."

"Sounds like a plan, but how will you get home?"

"I took the streetcar to your hotel, but I think I'll take Uber home. When I looked for information on New Orleans, people said they run erratically at night."

Jo couldn't recall visiting the Café on a previous visit to New Orleans and the beignets were the perfect dessert that also gave them a boost of energy as they sat at their final bar.

"What drink should we try here?" Jo asked.

"How about a Brandy Milk punch. It's supposed to be an iconic drink for this city, and I think it would complement the beignets."

They had their first taste of the drink and both thought it was delicious.

"I think if I lived here I would be thirty pounds heavier from drinking and eating. I think it must take some acclimating to run in this high humidity. I know that I start sweating profusely every time I step out in the heat of the day and it isn't even summer here."

"Yeah, when I stepped out of the airport this afternoon, it was a stark contrast to the fall weather back home in Green Bay. It was a crisp forty-five degrees there and that was after it warmed up from a temperature in the thirties overnight."

"I can just feel my grapevines dying with those cold temperatures, but it's a nice offset to the nighttime mugginess here. Let's get to work."

Soon there was the background noise of the bar and the French Quarter and the sound of the keys clacking under Jo's fingers. Jill was able to eliminate several of the farmers and by the time they were sipping their last swallow of the brandy milk punch, the two women had eliminated all but two farmers as having anything suspicious happening on their land. It was a variety of financial reports, data gathered from the local farmers' association, and other similar sources. Of course any of these farmers could have a personal reason to dispose of Mr. Cheval, but in this first round of investigation, nothing was screaming at her.

# CHAPTER 13

Jill was pleased to have no lingering effects from their bar tour the previous morning. She'd packed her bags and Alicia was going to drop her off at Nathan's hotel on her way to work. Jill promised to keep her updated on the investigation and to keep her in mind if she ever needed a second pathologist on one of her cases.

Jill made arrangements to meet with Briggs and Heyer as soon as she dropped her baggage off at the hotel bag check. She wondered what they would think of her drone idea. She would ask them questions to make sure she wasn't violating any airspace rules for the New Orleans airport.

She arrived at their station about an hour after she left Alicia's. Noting the time and an app on her phone, Nathan's plane was due to land in about ten minutes. The poor man would be tired from the red-eye flight.

"Do you have the address of the sample where our victim encountered the monster truck," Briggs asked. "I feel silly calling it the monster truck, but I can't think of anything else to call it as just a truck doesn't fit the what was described by Mr. Cheval."

"I do and I don't, and I have a solution," Jill said leaving the detectives frowning. "I researched the farm he sampled, and the owner of that field led me nowhere – nothing unusual about this farmer. So then I looked at the farms around this field to try and guess where the monster truck might have originated from and I ended up with twelve farms. Again my team member and I researched these twelve and eliminated all but two as having anything suspicious in their background. This doesn't preclude a motive for murder from another source like some kind of domestic dispute. Today, I'd like to hear about the results of the particular sample he took and my partner is arriving at the airport about now from California for business reasons and he's bringing my drone with him. I'd like to put the drone up in the air in the area of the field to see if I can spot the truck from the air. I wanted to check in with you guys as to whether you're aware of any drone regulations in New Orleans?"

"Whoa, slow down," said Briggs and, "back-up. You know exactly where the sample was taken which would be where the truck is sighted and you want us to contact Ms. Fontaine to find out what the testing revealed, correct?"

"Yes, if it does come back with Dicamba spray and the field owner didn't put it there we may have our source for a dispute between neighbors."

"Okay, I'll take that," said Heyer. "Are you telling us you'll be staying longer in the NOLA area as your partner has arrived from California?"

"Yes, but I forgot to ask him when he's due to return so I'm not sure how much longer I'll be here," Jill replied feeling dumb for not asking Nathan when his return trip was. She would need to change her return ticket as soon as possible.

She saw both Briggs and Heyer swallow and Jill wondered if that was a good sign or not.

"Don't you want my help for a few more days?" she asked with a cheeky grin.

Briggs sighed and said, "We'll need the farmer name of the

field so we can run him or her through our systems. As for the drone, explain what you're planning to do there."

"If this monster truck is as big as our victim described, it's unlikely that it's parked in a garage, although it might be in a barn. I'm hoping to spot it from the air so we can interview the owner."

"We do have our own drone in the department. We can't use it for spying on people or near the airport. Also, I believe the jurisdiction of this farmland lies in either Livingston or St. John the Baptist Parish so it would be beyond our jurisdiction to fly our drone there."

"You have a parish named St. John the Baptist?" Jill asked surprised by the use of a saint's name for a parish.

"Yes, we also have a football team named the Saints," Heyer said with a broad smile.

"Oh yeah, I forgot, the Saints. I'm a Green Bay Packers fan, so I forget at times that other cities have football teams that may be loved as much as we love our Packers."

"You're a Packers fan? Sorry about your quarterback and your season. When Drew Brees went down with a foot injury, our season was over that year," Heyer said.

"Yeah, our season has been terrible. We were first in our division then we had the QB injury and our backup QB needed to learn on the job, but what it's really spotlighted is how terrible our defense is. Aaron is such a brilliant quarterback that he can collect points to hide the defense's deficiencies. Though to be fair our backup has a lot of three and outs, and so it's a lot of time for the defense to be on the field."

"Can I just say that was an out of body experience?" Briggs said. "I've never been in the presence of two women talking football in detail. Yes, I've come across your species before, but only one at a time."

"You know that women buy over half of the NFL gear," Jill said.

"If I weren't a detective, I would be a sports writer for the Times-Picayune," Heyer said.

"Ladies I defer to your greater football knowledge. Can we get back to the case?"

"Sure, I gather you're suggesting that you lack probable cause to officially take your drone to the field in question. Is that correct?"

"Yes. I don't even know any law enforcement in that area that might turn a blind eye to our drone in the sky."

"Okay I have a remote airmen certificate to fly my drone. Perhaps my partner might want some fresh air today after the long flight and so could take it out to farming land to practice or to get a view of the Maurepas Swamp which is nearby, but we'd be safely away from alligators on the farmland."

"Those are reasonable excuses if someone tries to stop you out in farmland, but it could be dangerous, you are on the trail of a killer. Did you bring any weapons with you to New Orleans – pepper spray, perhaps?" Briggs asked.

"You must be testing my familiarity with the laws. No I didn't transport any kind of a weapon here. In California, I own no guns or pepper spray. The only knives I have are in the kitchen. I recently obtained a black belt in Tai Chi and my partner is a master black belt in Hapkido. When I was solving a case in Texas, I purchased a can of bug killer and used that in self-defense and perhaps I'll get one here. It's better than pepper spray as it has a longer reach."

"I don't know what to say to that explanation other than Dr. Quint, you're a person of many qualities."

"Okay it's all part of the job for me. I'll wait to hear back from you on the results of the plant test that Mr. Cheval performed as well as any new information you glean from Jayden's mother."

"Keep us posted as well. In fact, I think I'd like a call in from you every thirty minutes until you notify me that you're back in the city of New Orleans. I don't know why but I have a bad feeling about you visiting the farm fields today," Heyer requested.

"Will do," Jill replied and left the detective division. This time she took a different path through the French Quarter towards Nathan's hotel. She liked how each street seemed to represent a different adventure of sorts in learning about its history, architecture, and businesses. She thought that Nathan was likely at the hotel and sure enough he was at the registration desk checking in.

She walked up to him and placing a hand on his back stood on her toes to kiss the side of his face. He had a sexy five o'clock shadow as he hadn't shaved yet today. He soon received his room cards and a bellman indicated that Jill's luggage would be sent up to their room.

# CHAPTER 14

$\mathcal{A}$n hour later, they had their lives and plans sorted out. Nathan wanted to go with her to the farmland, and fortunately there was a car rental agency associated with the hotel and they soon had a vehicle to take them there. After a brief stint to brush his teeth, shave, shower and change clothes, he was ready to follow Jill's latest adventure. Like the detectives, he thought the story of the monster truck a little far-fetched. He also knew his superior martial arts skills and their rental car would be unable to withstand the crunching power of a monster truck. Then there was the issue of the gun mounted in the truck bed.

Jill tested her drone inside the hotel room while Nathan was getting ready. He'd picked an older hotel with high ceilings which gave her more space to practice her craft. They decided beforehand that if a big truck approached they would quickly get in their car and head for the highway. The truck likely was not street safe and would lack cornering maneuverability. While Jill flew the drone, Nathan would watch for the approach of any vehicles. If she had to, she could operate the drone from the car if they had to make a quick getaway. It flew up to 100mph and surely they wouldn't be going that fast in the rental car. Besides if she was lucky, she'd find the truck parked and would know in advance if anyone started it up.

She looked at Nathan as they left in the rental car and said, "You ready for another adventure?"

"No, but I've accepted living on the edge with you. This is an uncommon enemy in that if the monster truck is real, it could squash us like bugs. At least your detective friends know where to look for our bodies. I'm glad they made you report in every thirty minutes. At least the cavalry will come for our bodies."

"My, aren't you an optimistic soul today. It must be because you're tired from the overnight flight."

Jill handed him a mug of coffee and set about locating the farm based on geographic coordinates on an app she downloaded back at the hotel. She'd never tried finding a destination that way before. It seemed to work like any other mapping software and it looked like it would take about thirty to forty minutes to arrive at their destination.

Looking out the window she said, "It's so flat and green here, and I bet when we get out of the car, we'll hear insects buzzing."

"They're probably celebrating right now with the excitement of your arrival. I bet they can smell you coming and can't wait to sink their fangs into your delicious blood."

"Thanks for that visual, but I fear you're right, and I didn't apply any bug spray this morning, so there'll probably be swarms of them when I get out of the car. Ugh. Then I'll look like I have chicken pox by the end of the day with welts. Someday when I'm bored, I should experiment with my blood to find out why it's so attractive to insects. At least I don't generally have problems with bees. Tell me about the winery you're visiting here."

"Actually, it's a distillery."

"Rum?"

"No, gin, vodka, and absinthe."

"Wow, you could have fun with those labels and now you have the trifecta of the label business – wine, beer, and spirits. Congratulations sweetie!"

"Yeah, I'm pleased. The contract I signed with this owner was for a lot less money than usual, but I had many reasons for wanting to work with this owner. I hope I don't live to regret my decision."

"You're pretty good at sizing up owners. I think all of the owners you don't like have been with you a long time. So either you were looking for their business as you were starting out as an artist, or you hadn't had enough experience to develop the owner-meter in your mind yet."

"True and the only thing that keeps me from firing those owners is a sense of loyalty to them for helping me build a reputation in my business."

"So what did you like about this owner?"

"He's in a part of the country in which I have no clients, and he has a small production and is an artist himself. He wants to migrate from his current design of classic New Orleans symbols like the fleur-de-lis to perhaps a more European design. As more distilleries open in the New Orleans area, part of the way to separate himself from them is to make his label different. So we're meeting tomorrow."

"That sounds artistically exciting melding the new and the old. I bet you'll design a fantastic new label for him!"

"If we survive the monster truck today."

"We will. We're really good at avoiding death."

They had been driving through agriculture fields for the past ten minutes. They were south of the Mississippi River with mostly farm fields and few homes.

"We're coming up to our destination, slow down as these numbers change fast," Jill said looking at her phone.

"Stop. This is it."

Jill had pre-assembled the drone so they could make a quick entrance and exit to the farmland. Their goal was to be out there for less than five minutes. They were surrounded by farm lands and despite being a botanist she hadn't thought to look up what a soybean plant looked like. She knew what a bean plant looked like, but given that she had the geocoordinates she assumed she was looking at soybeans. Looking around she couldn't tell where a monster truck might come from, so she set about to get a 360-degree view of her location. The drone was up, camera recording and transmitting to the cloud and she went out as far as she could which was about one-thousand feet or three acres. She spun it around and captured about half of what she needed. So much for looking for a truck, she was moving at such a dizzying speed she couldn't stop to identify shapes on the ground. Fortunately, she'd be able to slow it down once she got back to the hotel.

"Babe, we have a problem, it's time to go," she heard Nathan say calmly.

"Okay," she said walking back to the car continuing her movement of the drone, she'd now captured another ninety degrees with the final quarter to go. She heard a loud motor in her vicinity but didn't want to take her eyes off the drone. She got in the car planning to bring the drone back to the car and lower it through the sunroof. She checked it out at the hotel to make sure it fit and it would. She kept her eyes on the drone as Nathan started the car.

"Babe we have another problem," he said knowing that Jill hadn't taken her eyes off of the drone screen to assess her surroundings. "The monster truck has arrived and it's blocking our exit from this one-way street."

"Oh," she said looking up and doing a quick assessment. "What if I bring the drone down and crash it right in front of the truck and then I'll act like a witless dumb blonde."

"This I got to see. You're usually a failure at acting stupid, but I'm guessing our lives are on the line so have a go at it. I'm going to text your detective that we're in trouble."

"Goodbye Lucy, it was a short but fruitful life," she said and then guided the drone right in front of the moving monster truck, and she saw it get crushed under its wheels.

"Lucy? You named your drone Lucy?"

"Yeah as in 'Lucy in the sky with diamonds', that fabulous Beatles song. It seemed to fit her. I just destroyed a five hundred dollar drone all in the effort to prove we're guileless tourists practicing our flying."

Nathan had used Jill's phone to reach the detective on a video call. He'd been worried from the get-go about Jill's harebrained scheme and had checked in with the detectives to assure himself that they could reach him via video call if necessary. If he was going to die by a monster truck, he wanted a video of it for the police.

They were at a standstill as the monster truck blocked their progress back to the highway. The truck was indeed a monster, it was so high that Jill and Nathan were looking at tires and the shock absorber underbody of the truck. They could not a see a driver or passenger or what might be in the truck bed. Nathan had the phone facing out of the windshield with Detective Briggs observing from his end. Meanwhile, Jill reached over and honked the horn making both Nathan and the detective jump at the sound. Still, the truck stood tall blocking their way like a twelve-foot high growling Rottweiler.

Nathan studied the road wondering if they could make a run for it on the crop side. There was a little bit of easement and he'd bet the big truck couldn't corner that fast. He hoped he wouldn't blow it. He waited another minute and the truck just sat there engine revving, massive tires looking threatening. He said to the detective and Jill. "Keep your fingers crossed I'm going to make a run for the side of the truck." Nathan passed Jill her phone and studied the road. His side had a ditch, but Jill's was gently sloped. He hoped his vision was correct about that as he'd noticed many pools of standing water since traveling to this destination. The only thing worse than being squished by the truck was being covered in one of those pools of vermin-infested water just before you were squished.

Then he floored the vehicle and they slid by the monster truck before it could react to block them. Nathan concentrated on driving, and Jill looked out the back window to see if they gave chase.

They did not. The truck was not moving. When they cleared the truck by a safe range, they ended the call with the detective. With the promise to come straight into the station.

"Maybe they didn't see us move," Jill proposed. "The cab is so high they don't have good visibility."

"That's a fantasy. I think this was an effort to intimidate us or perhaps the people in the truck knew it had crushed your drone and their work was done. Is there anyone in the truck bed? "

"No. In the story my victim told to his friend, there were one or two men in the back of the bed with mounted rifles and the man pulled out what the victim thought was going to be a sidearm, but was instead a cell phone and took his picture. The truck is so high that we can't see if there is a gun mount that's empty at the moment. Also, the monster truck kicked up a lot of dust so they must not have come on this road as it's paved. I can't wait to see my footage and while I mourn Lucy's death, I'm glad I paid extra for the technology to transmit the video to the cloud."

"I hope it worked. I'd hate to have Lucy die in vain," Nathan said with a relaxed smile now that they were beyond the monster truck. They still had roads to cover before getting back to New Orleans but they wouldn't get stuck on any other one way roads from here on out.

Jill had used her cell phone to dial into the drone's cloud site. She was just looking for a hint of video coverage which she found despite the poor cell tower coverage in the area. They headed back to the hotel and Jill gathered up her laptop for the walk with

Nathan to the police station. He hadn't been to New Orleans before, but immediately liked what he saw on their walk through the French Quarter. Jill pointed out a few sights she had come to know including the carousel bar that she and Jo visited.

97

# CHAPTER 15

*J*ill was directed to the detectives' division and she soon introduced Nathan to Briggs and Heyer.

"That was quite an adventure you had out there," Heyer said. "I would say that it didn't meet our standards of southern hospitality."

"We ran a search on the vehicle from the picture you sent us, but as you can imagine as the vehicle isn't street legal, there's no registration," Briggs said. "I wasn't surprised by that finding."

Jill looked at Nathan impressed that he thought to send the detectives a picture when she hadn't. She grinned to herself that Nathan was becoming a good detective and a part of her team whether he wanted to or not.

"Are you able to monitor police traffic in other jurisdictions?" Jill asked.

"Why?" Detective Heyer asked.

"I just wondered if a complaint was made to the police of the jurisdiction that that farm was located in to complain about someone flying a drone. Just a curiosity question."

"I'll look into it. Let's look at your footage, sorry about your drone."

"Yeah, me too. It was a great tool for surveying my vineyard from the air. You can see different problems. I'm going to miss Lucy."

"Lucy?" Asked Heyer, puzzled.

"Don't ask. It's her drone's name."

Detective Heyer didn't entirely drop her puzzled look, but they moved on to look at Jill's laptop and then she had to look away.

"Wow, that's a nauseating speed in the air. Can you slow it down?" Heyer asked.

"Yes," replied Jill manipulating the controls and the video footage slowed significantly. "I flew it at one-hundred miles an hour as we feared the appearance of the monster truck. I knew I could slow it down later. I got about three acres around the field in question and I guess I got around 300 of the 360-degree circle before Lucy met her death. Maybe the monster truck didn't chase us because it thought it had destroyed the drone, but I honked at it and it wouldn't move so who knows."

"Jill, has anyone ever trained you in avoiding antagonizing bad people?" Briggs asked. "Police are trained in something called HRT or Hostage Rescue Team and I can assure that honking a car horn is not in our playbook."

"That's why I was there," Nathan muttered under his breath.

Briggs looked at him and gave him a look of sympathy.

"I was just trying to play my role as a dumb tourist, mad that I crashed my drone. Too bad the driver missed the rest of my performance. I should add that we don't know if this is the same monster truck that encountered Mr. Cheval. I remember in our conversation with Keith that Julien said there was a cloud of dust kicked up by the monster truck, and we were on an asphalt surface with no dust."

"I took a couple of pictures of the truck so we have that for your records," Nathan said, and Jill beamed at him with approval. He just raised his eyebrows back at her.

The four of them stared at the slowed video of the drone. Jill sat back and said, "I don't know what I'm looking for, but nothing looks odd on this surveillance."

"I agree with you, but maybe I'll send it to our crime lab guys to see if they see something unusual," Heyer said.

Jill had been so busy that morning with moving her luggage, operating the drone and the two visits to the detectives, that she hadn't checked her email. After copying the drone footage onto a flash drive for the detectives, she glanced at her email to see if Jo had discovered anything.

She opened an email from her from about an hour ago and read:

*'I was curious about those two companies we couldn't identify last night, and you know me I love a good business challenge. So as I sat in the seminar this morning, I did some more research and still didn't find anything which is very unusual for an American farmer. So then I thought of a recent scandal called the Paradise Papers which were a result of some computer hacker getting into the files of a law firm and exposing large companies with their off-shore tax havens, but again no trace of the corporation there. I'll keep looking, but I would advise you concentrate on that farm as it's the only one that's suspicious.'*

Jill finished Jo's email and decided to keep the contents to herself as there was nothing yet to report to the detectives. She wanted to study the video herself one more time to see if when she was focused, she might see something unusual. She looked over at Nathan who seemed to be drooping; likely his red-eye flight was catching up with him after the crash from the adrenaline rush over the encounter with the monster truck.

"Unless you detectives want my input on something, I think we're done for the day. I do plan to watch the tape another time, but I can't think of anything more to do on this case at this moment in time."

"We appreciate your help and the sacrifice of Lucy. I'll let you know if our lab comes up with anything. Meanwhile we have an appointment to talk to Mr. Cheval's son and the child's mother. We also have a message in to Ms. Fontaine seeking the results of the sample Mr. Cheval took during the first interaction with the monster truck. We asked yesterday about that and still don't have an answer from her office."

A few minutes later Jill and Nathan were walking through the French Quarter again on the way back to their hotel. There was a little more activity in the bars along the way and Jill had made a slight detour to a restaurant that Alicia had taken her to that had been serving Po'boy sandwiches since 1950. It wasn't a fancy place, but Jill liked their food and figured that one of the sandwiches would sit well with Nathan and likely help put him to sleep.

"This feels like a pizza parlor given the level of noise in here," Nathan said.

"Yes, but it doesn't smell like pizza does it?"

"No, and I think that's due to a wide variety of ingredients in their sandwiches. They have some fishy smelling fish on the menu and yet I can see you're content with what is essentially a grilled cheese sandwich."

"Yeah, you know I don't like many varieties of seafood and even less as a sandwich, but clearly I'm in the minority. I thought you would be conflicted between catfish and alligator sausage which sounds gross to me, but I can see you love the alligator."

"It's not something you find at home. We don't have alligators and while I've had catfish in California, it's not revered like it is here and certainly I haven't had Cajun cooking. I can see I'm really going to enjoy eating here."

"There's a shop a few blocks over that sells all kinds of sauces that are specific to this region. I tried a few of their hot sauces just to confirm that I don't like hot sauce and I don't."

Nathan laughed at Jill's persistence at proving to herself that she didn't like some foods. She'd come around on avocados, but pretty much had not moved on any other of her food hates.

They finished their lunch and continued a few blocks back to the hotel. When they entered the hotel room, Jill felt like crying when she saw the empty drone case. At least Lucy had died valiantly, now Jill had to find something unique in that footage while Nathan got a few hours of sleep.

He settled into bed, and Jill took her laptop down to the hotel restaurant where she could make noise and talk to herself without disrupting Nathan's sleep. With a diet cola at her side, she again watched the video footage and again saw nothing that peaked her interest. How else could she look at the tape? She could study buildings and vehicles, or perhaps crops. The trouble with studying crops was she didn't know the appearance of some of the Louisiana crops. Today, she'd taken a guess on soybeans, but what did cotton or tobacco plants look like?

On her next run through the video, she broke the screen up in a grid and this forced her to examine and identify every blip on the video. Her camera on the drone took thirty frames per second or about nine-thousand frames of video. By her calculations, she needed to study about every hundredth frame or so, but ninety was a lot and she'd leave that to the New Orleans crime lab; they probably had a software package that made this kind of analysis easier. So she did some more calculation and backed that up with video study, she could study every nine-hundredth frame and collect all of the details. With this in mind, she studied homes, cars, tractors, and barns. Interestingly, there were no people out in the fields. Jill wondered if it was the growing cycle of the crops or just a time of day thing. She noted that she didn't see where the monster truck had come from and if it weren't for Nathan's quick thinking they wouldn't have a record of it.

Her eyes were straining with her study of the minute detail and the seemingly unchanging view. She stood up and stretched and walked a little before sitting back down. She needed to find something in this footage, she hadn't wanted Lucy the drone, to die in vain. She was on her third pass when she noticed something on a farm plot devoted to corn. She slowed the video way down and looked at it in at least ten different areas of the same field. She would enlarge the frame compare the plant to pictures of the plant she thought it was and then move on to the next frame. The cornfield produced between $6,000 and $7,000 in grain sales, but between the rows of corn was a crop that brought in $3.2M by her calculations and that was enough to kill for. She looked for additional corn fields in the footage she had and her phone rang making her jump at the interruption to her concentration.

"This is Jill," she said into the phone still staring intently at the video footage.

"Hello Jill, this is Professor Watson from UC Davis regarding your evergreen question."

"Oh, hi Dr. Watson. Do you have an answer to my nutmeg question?"

"Yes I do and can I say that my students had a great time testing your idea if nutmeg could be made tasteless yet still retain its poisonous properties. The answer is yes it can."

The professor took several minutes to explain the experiment she'd designed with the students. They had even gone so far as to feed one of their lab rats the concoction they created and they noticed the effects of the poison on the rat. Best of all according to the professor she and her students had new information thanks to the experiment and they could publish the results in a botany journal. Jill paused for a moment and then asked what she thought would be the first question the detectives had about these findings:

"Would you testify in court about your experiment and its results if the detectives need you to explain how it's possible to poison someone with nutmeg?"

"I've never been called for my scientific opinion on a botany matter. As long as the police department paid my travel there, I would testify about this experiment with nutmeg. Do you think they'll make that request?"

"I don't know. I don't know how the court system works in Louisiana. If they give me a sense that they'll be asking you in future to testify I'll drop you an email relaying that information."

"Thanks that's all I can ask. You have a good day Dr. Quint."

Jill ended the call and was about to call the detectives when she saw Nathan walking toward her looking refreshed from his nap.

He sat down next to her grabbing her glass for a swig of diet cola.

"You're looking chipper. I think the nap must've done you a lot of good."

"It did. Just before I put my head on the pillow, I felt like I was walking around in a slightly dizzy fog and now my mind is clear. Did you discover anything while I was asleep?"

"I discovered lots of things when you were sleep. I'm wondering how the detectives will take some of this information as I think the police in the parish in which that field is located might be involved."

Nathan looked at her puzzled and asked, "Are you suggesting that one or more police personnel located in that parish might be crooked?"

"Maybe, then again I had to look a few times at the crop to realize what it is. I don't know how big this parish is or how much their law enforcement knows each and every farm field and that parish is just a question in the back of my mind."

"What's the crop that you're suspicious about?"

# CHAPTER 16

"Marijuana. After the umpteenth time that I stared at that video, I finally noticed something growing between each row of corn. I enlarged the picture and searched different parts of the cornfield to confirm my finding of marijuana. Guess what an acre of marijuana sells for on the market," Jill asked.

"I guess it depends on whether it's legally or illegally in the state. If it's an illegal crop, I would guess it's at least ten times the price of what it would be if it were a legal crop."

"It also depends on what state you're growing hemp in. Turns out in Washington, many farmers are facing bankruptcy as the taxes are high and the demand not what they expected. In California, some farmers are hoping to buy out the Washington farms for expansion. Louisiana is a conservative state and it has approved marijuana for medical reasons only. It proposes to grow its marijuana on college campuses hoping that that will be the way the state can control the production of hemp and help the schools with revenue from medical marijuana sales. It's an interesting concept. Bottom line is this cornfield with marijuana in it is illegal."

"What did the detective say about that?"

"I haven't told him yet is I had just finished discovering the crop. Then my expert from UC Davis called with news about nutmeg. So now I have two things to report on and I was just about to call them and you walked up. Let me make this call and then we can decide what we want to do with the rest of the day. I'm not sure there is additional work for me on this case at this point."

"Have you identified the owner of that acre?"

"No, Jo is taking the lead to find out who the owner is and surprisingly she's not having success. She then resorted to the Paradise Papers created by the International Consortium of Investigative Journalists, but I haven't heard the results of that research yet."

"What are the Paradise Papers?"

"Last year a hacker got into the files of this law firm in the Cayman Islands. This particular firm does a lot of secret corporations to hide from public view the assets of people like Queen Elizabeth, the U.S. Secretary of Commerce, several Presidents and Premiers of countries around the world. The hackers walked away with this huge data dump that journalists around the world could use for research."

Nathan looked worried and said, "This case is taking on a life of its own. Weren't you called here because someone died from evil spirits and now you think someone involved in the Paradise Papers might be involved in this case? I think it's time to pack your bags and head home to California."

"It is starting to look far more sinister than it did when I was standing over Mr. Cheval in the autopsy suite. Let me call the detectives."

Jill reached them in their car as they were returning to the office after interviewing Jayden Cheval's mother. They agreed to swing by the hotel to look at Jill's conclusions.

"Sorry but it looks like we'll have to delay our plans for a little bit while I talk to the detectives. The nice thing about New Orleans is that in many ways it's a twenty-four seven city."

"Don't worry about it. I'm far more concerned about your safety given who might be your opponent in this case. If Jo does find a connection to the Paradise Papers, then your opponent is likely filthy rich. You're driving me to drink so I'm going to go have a discussion with the bartender and see if I can find a local drink I should try."

"That sounds like an excellent idea. If nothing piques your interest, try a mint julep. I know that's a drink native to Kentucky, but it's a southern drink and mint sounds good on a hot, muggy day."

He gave her a thumbs up and headed toward the bar. She was sitting in the lobby of the hotel and had found a quiet corner to do her research. Now she stood up both to stretch her muscles and to be on the lookout for the two detectives. She saw them enter the lobby and waved her arms to catch their attention.

She decided she tell them about the nutmeg first.

"My botany contact at UC Davis confirmed it's possible to make nutmeg tasteless but still in a high enough concentration to kill. She's going to get a scientific paper out of our question and so if this case goes to trial, she's willing to be your botany expert should you need one. Here's her business information to pass on to the attorneys at the appropriate time."

"Okay thanks for running this down for us," Heyer said. "What did you discover from your drone footage that has you on edge?"

"I'm going to play a part of the footage for you and see if you can detect what's wrong with this picture. It took me three tries to see the problem, but since you're detectives, I'm sure you'll be much faster than me."

Both detectives gave her raised eyebrows but then settled in to watch the video, just as they hit repeat, Nathan arrived with their drinks.

"Would you detectives like me to fetch you something from

the bar? I know you're on duty, but they do have soft drinks or Shirley Temples."

"I'll pass on the Shirley Temple, but my partner and I would love any kind of diet soda," Heyer said and Nathan made his second journey to the bar.

On the second pass through the field, Jill knew that Briggs had seen the problem when he commanded, "Freeze the frame."

Heyer continued to stare, but Jill could see she didn't recognize the problem.

Briggs looked at Jill and said, "I did a stint in narcotics before I became a detective, Heyer here missed that particular hell. We see what looks to be an entire acre planted with corn as we would expect, and marijuana between the rows of corn. That crop might have a street value of three to four million."

Heyer got closer and stared intently at the picture. "You're right, I know nothing of narcotics other than what I came across as a patrol officer or learned about in the police academy. Certainly, I've never seen it growing in a field and I might've looked at it as either a weed, and isn't that ironic as it is a weed, or I might've thought that it was mint, like that leaf in your drink Jill."

Looking at Detective Briggs, Jill asked, "I think this marijuana is being grown in the open. If law enforcement had ever driven down that street, they would've seen the crop and wondered at it? Right?"

"Did you see it when you got out of your car with the drone?" Briggs asked.

"No, but then I think I was so worried about some hulking monster truck that I was blind to my surroundings when we pulled up to the field. Besides if I were a pot grower, I would put a stock of corn at the end of the row to hide the marijuana behind it. Let me try Google Earth to see if I can see the plants from the street."

Jill did so, but the crop that was there was very different from the alternating rows of corn and marijuana. "That looks like a soybean plant so that must've been what was planted at the time that Google plotted this part of the world."

Jill then pulled out a Google forum, and they could see that the company had no plans to visit Louisiana to update their maps in the near future.

"The other problem with this plot of land is I haven't been able to identify who owns it."

"That's simple we can just find that out from the parish tax records."

"Good luck with that, I couldn't find tax records through my searches. I also did another search on owners of acreage in that area and there are two corporations that teammates and I have been unable to identify."

"I want to get our ducks in order on this. It's not as though someone can make an entire crop of marijuana disappear. They could cultivate the corn and marijuana but from your footage of the field, it's not ready and they would destroy the value of both. I think our monster truck has something to do with protecting that crop and since you crashed your drone into it, they more than likely think you lost any film it was collecting," Briggs said.

"Okay, what do you think about the motive for this case? The sample that Mr. Cheval took was not from the corn and marijuana acre and I think he was looking for drift of Dicamba. If that was his premise, why kill him?" Jill asked. "I did some research online, and Dicamba can't be used on marijuana – it kills the plant. So the farmer had nothing to worry about from Mr. Cheval."

"Is there some other product that you would use on marijuana that you wouldn't on soybeans?" Heyer asked.

"Good question, I'll have to do more research. Did you find out what the test results were on the soybean field?"

"That's kind of weird also. Ms. Fontaine was unable to find a record that our victim submitted a sample for testing," Briggs said.

"Yes, but Keith Townsend mentioned that not only had our victim submitted one sample, but he also went back and got another. We know this because Keith volunteered to do it for him. So Ms. Fontaine is saying two samples are missing from the state's database? That's curious."

"This is about as strange a murder case as I've ever seen," Heyer said. "Between the nutmeg poisoning, the monster truck, missing field samples, and now a marijuana field owned by a mysterious person, this feels like something big is swirling around here."

Jill nodded and said, "I'm not sure how much more I can do to help. My friend is still working on identifying the corporation, and I'll look for a pesticide or herbicide that's used to benefit marijuana but is bad for soybeans. I don't think that knowledge will get us very far with this case as it won't point to the murderer, but I'll say this. If your suspect could reach in and alter state computers, then you are up against someone who's very powerful."

Shortly they said their goodbyes and Jill switched gears and asked Nathan what he wanted to do.

"I'd like to visit the distillery I'm going to tomorrow to see its current state, then let's take in the music, food, and ambiance of the French Quarter."

# CHAPTER 17

*J*ill and Nathan found themselves seated at a distillery drinking vodka. Jill couldn't distinguish between a good and bad vodka, but Nathan liked what he tasted. Jill decided to try the absinthe after she got a promise from Nathan that if she started doing anything stupid, that he would take her back to their hotel until she was sober. She watched the bartender pour her drink over a cube of sugar knowing that the pouring experience was part of the aura of absinthe.

"What's the alcohol content of this drink?" Jill asked.

"Let me read the bottle," Nathan said reaching for the bottle on the bar. "74 percent."

"Oh. Definitely stop me when I climb up on the bar and try to sing Adele's 'Hello'. My off-key notes will bust the glasses in here."

Nathan chuckled and said, "Are you kidding? I'll be applauding you and filming your performance for prosperity."

Jill wrinkled her nose and tapped her glass to his and said, "Cheers".

They finished their drinks and left to move on to a French restaurant for dinner. They followed that with a visit to a jazz club. Nathan enjoyed jazz and often listened to it while he was designing. Jill on the other hand, was utterly unmoved by jazz but she enjoyed watching people's expressions while they grooved to the music. Jill was doing her slow sweep of the crowd and paused at one face. Hadn't she seen that face before? She was staring at the face of a woman that she had seen elsewhere recently, but where?

Nathan picked up on her zeroing in on someone. It was like his body was attuned to Jill's brain going on high power to figure something out. He knew she didn't like jazz music, but until a minute ago she'd been having fun scanning the crowd watching others enjoy the music.

He leaned in and asked, "What's up? Something has caught your attention."

"There's a woman over there that I've seen elsewhere tonight. I'm just trying to puzzle where."

Nathan followed Jill's gaze to the woman in question. She was seated at the bar, by herself, in conversation with no one.

He also recognized that he'd seen her before. He looked away and whispered, "I know what you mean. I've seen her before as well."

He focused on the music for a while then put his arm around Jill's shoulder and said into her ear, "She was on the street near the distillery, and she had her back to us at the restaurant. Until she turned around just now I didn't recognize that back of a customer in the restaurant. What are the odds that we would find her in all three places we've been tonight?"

Jill pulled out her smartphone looked up a few things on Google and then replied, "Four-hundred to one. We take the total number of distilleries in the French Quarter, then account for the number of restaurants and music venues. We're being followed. Is she armed?"

Nathan studied the smooth lines of the woman's clothing, and replied, "I don't know what's in her purse, or if she might have an ankle holster or knife on her body."

"I'm going to go talk to her," Jill said. "I'm sure I won't get any answers, but at least I'll know something more about her."

"Want me to do that? I could flirt with her and see what I learn."

Jill didn't think it would be that easy but said, "Go ahead and see what you find out."

Jill watched him approach the woman with her back turned to them. Her eyes moved to the liquor shelves and she noticed some mirrored glass behind the bottles. She bet the woman was watching them in the mirror. She had to see Nathan's approach. Jill decided she'd let Nathan work his magic without her supervision and instead let her glance roam the remainder of the music lovers. She recognized no other faces, but did come across a man staring at her. She stared back trying to figure out why he was watching her over everyone else in the venue. He faded back into the crowd as he noticed Jill staring and she was too slow thinking of using her phone to capture the image of the people focused on them.

She returned her gaze to Nathan and guessed he wasn't making much progress based on his body language. He seemed stiff and no longer had his hand on the women's back. He said a few more words to the woman and then returned to Jill.

"This is a weird night. First, my girlfriend encourages me to go flirt with another woman and then it turns out it's not a woman."

A snort burst out of Jill and she said, "Whoops, how could I have been wrong about that?"

"You? Heck, I was right there with you thinking that was the woman we saw earlier tonight. That is a 'no' on both accounts. He said that he wasn't at the location we were at earlier and he was watching us as he was trying to decide which one of us was more attractive to him. Apparently, he swings either way."

"Oh."

"Yes, oh."

"You did tell him that we are in love with each other and not looking for a third party?"

"Yeah I did, but I must say this was one of my unusual days in my life. I rarely take red-eyes, encounter monster trucks, consult with detectives, watch you drink absinthe, and hit on a man. Maybe this is all a dream, and I'll wake up in my bed in Palisades Valley, California. Pinch me and maybe I'll awaken from this nightmare."

Jill smiled at Nathan's comments and leaned over to pat him, "You poor man. Let's look at the day another way. You joined your girlfriend in New Orleans, took a drive in the country, had a chance to practice car maneuverability, chatted with two New Orleans natives, enjoyed walking through the French Quarter, had an excellent nap, got creative ideas for your meeting with a new client, ate a wonderful French meal, and passed the evening enjoying jazz music."

"That must be the absinthe talking," Nathan replied.

Jill just leaned over to kiss Nathan forgetting the man at the bar and the other gentleman she thought had been watching them earlier. They were tired from their adventurous day. They lounged in their chairs a while longer before departing the jazz club for their hotel. It was early by New Orleans standards, but they were tired and ready to end it. They had a five block uneventful walk back to their hotel.

# CHAPTER 18

The next morning Jill found Nathan up at an early hour for him. He'd been thinking of his travels around the French Quarter and Louisiana in terms of his new client's needs. The client wanted to keep some of the old and merge with fresh ideas. Specifically, he no longer wanted association with Disney-like pirates on his labels but instead wanted some other symbol that represented New Orleans. Their previous evening had given Nathan a wealth of ideas that might work to achieve this end and he was sketching them down as fast as he could out of fear they might disappear from his mind. After a quiet breakfast, they parted ways; he to meet with the new client and she to visit the Garden District. She wanted to view the Lafayette Cemetery and one or two historic houses. Overall Jill found cemeteries to be a waste of space. Occasionally they were impressive at getting a point across like all of the white crosses at any military cemetery, or Arlington National Cemetery where Revolutionary War graves were available to view and honor. In visiting Lafayette, she wasn't sure what she was supposed to see other than a lot of graves.

Just as she was leaving the hotel to make her way towards the cemetery, she got a text from Jo saying she was bored and what was she up to at the moment as she might join her? Jill mentioned the cemetery and Jo said she was game to explore it.

After arriving at the cemetery from the St. Charles streetcar, Jill waited for Jo to arrive by taxi and they entered the cemetery. And then her imagination took over. Her first thoughts were of the various hurricanes that had struck the city and how rising water level caused some bodies to float away. Where possible, the dead were buried above ground in mausoleums to ensure the safety of the deceased. She thought back to her days as a county coroner and what it had to be like to have well-preserved corpses floating with the newly dead in ravaged waters.

"Is there anyone famous buried here?" Jo asked.

"I don't think so, it might be the oldest cemetery in New Orleans and there are some unique mausoleums here. It's weird to be here - a place of dead bodies when you've been in charge of one-hundred dead bodies, just not buried, dead bodies."

"I was just thinking how weird it had to be during hurricanes here, when dead bodies would float out of cemeteries. You would have the newly dead floating with the preserved dead. As a pathologist would you instantly recognize that someone was preserved?"

"That's a good question. I'd like to think I would quickly recognize the difference because of the skin color and texture, but I'll admit I've never been confronted with that choice."

They arrived at a monument dedicated to the volunteer fire department and another for boys without parents.

"Are they still having funerals here?" Jo asked.

"Yes," and they stopped puzzled by a 'for sale' sign on one of the mausoleums.

"That's weird. What happens to the bodies already buried there? Why would you sell your family crypt?" Jo asked.

"I don't know. I've never been in a cemetery where a filled space was for sale. Let me look that up on google."

They stood in front of the sign while Jill read.

"Okay, there are a variety of reasons for selling the family plot. I guess you move the plaque with the names on it from the front to the sides or back when you sell. So it must happen frequently since there are rules for it. Do you and your kids want to be buried here? Are you thinking of buying it?" Jill asked with a small smile, pretty sure that she could guess Jo's thoughts on funeral arrangements.

"I can think of few things that are a bigger waste of money than being buried like this. My kids know to have me cremated and scatter my ashes on the Fox River bike trail so I'll have lots of company from bicyclists. How about you? Are you thinking of buying?"

"Hell no. My final testament states to have me cremated and I'd love to have my ashes sprinkled on the Burn Out ski trail at Northstar, but it will take a skier to carry out that wish for me. So I'll need to know a younger skier when I die at 103. I do like this cemetery though, I can just imagine the dead talking to each other and partying after dark when the public leaves."

"Seriously, your imagination is just plain weird considering you're a forensic pathologist and have spent more time around the dead than just about anyone else other than a mortician. Where to next?"

"I thought we'd walk through the Garden District and stare at the big southern mansions. There's one open to raise funds for the Opera Guild so we could learn about southern mansions."

"Sounds like a plan."

They were in the back corner of the cemetery and they saw dark clouds overhead so Jill paused to look at the weather report to see if they were about to get drenched. She had an umbrella, but if it was about to pour, then they'd have to cut short their tour.

They felt a shower of rain hit them, but then they quickly realized it was mortar dust from a nearby mausoleum hitting them. They both opened their mouths to say something while staring at the statue of a Madonna holding a child, then they saw another puff of dust ping off the statue. They both made a grab for each other as they ducked behind another crypt.

"Dammit, who is shooting at you, Jill?"

Jill thought of asking her how she knew the shot was intended for her, but she knew Jo was right.

"Probably the same person who tried to scare Nathan and I with a monster truck."

"A monster truck?" Jo whispered trying to see where the gun was.

"It's a long story involving a three million dollar crop of marijuana," Jill whispered back trying to see where the shots were coming from and guessing where she and Jo should run. She dialed 9-1-1 and informed the operator that an active shooter was in the cemetery. Jill and Jo conferred on where to go next, deciding they would run toward a nearby mausoleum as it looked like they could hide behind it and slowly make their way out of the cemetery. Again they were hit by dust, but it didn't feel as though any bullets had come close to them.

"Where do you think the shots are coming from?" Jo asked.

"It feels like someone is outside of the cemetery on a rooftop. Let's stay low and make our way to the entrance. Maybe another visitor is being shot at and not us."

Over the loud sound of approaching sirens Jo said, "You don't really believe that! You're spiking my bullshit meter."

Jill just smiled at her as they heard the arrival of the police squad cars outside the cemetery.

An hour later, they had their answer. The only gunshot damage to the cemetery monuments was in the area where Jill and Jo had been standing and indeed the crime scene team thought the shooting had occurred from a nearby rooftop of a vacant home undergoing restoration. The shooter was long gone at this point and the question was what to do next.

"I need to be back at my seminar in about ninety minutes. Let's grab a bite to eat across the street – maybe we'll luck out and they'll seat us without a reservation, I've heard it's one of the best restaurants in New Orleans."

They were brimming over with luck that day as they secured a table for lunch and since they had twenty-five cent martinis on the lunch menu, they were soon toasting their luck that day. Jo had the Caribbean curried shrimp while Jill ordered the wild-flower honey glazed gulf fish. They also ordered dessert knowing that since they were in one of the finest restaurants in Louisiana, they should try the creole cheesecake and the spiced peach and bourbon gateau.

"I was fed up with helping you with cases while we were in Scotland. Mostly I think because I'd wanted a relaxing vacation and I was mourning Nick's death. Now I've come around to a new way of thinking."

"What's that?" Jill asked fully aware that she thought she might be losing Jo's help with future cases.

"We really do good work as a team and there's always a victim left behind that our work brings solace for. I should have seen that way back with our second case. Henrik has turned into such a nice friend and we wouldn't have met him or have helped him reach peace over the death of his wife. In this case, we have a mother and a seven-year old boy who will find peace when we find the reason for your victim's murder. It's honorable work and I'm humbled that my knowledge of accounting can help people around the world. We're helping people where it matters – in their hearts."

This was such a surprising and unusual speech for Jo that it brought tears to Jill's eyes and she jumped up and walked around the table to give her friend a hug whispering, "Thank you."

Then they snapped apart recognizing the awkwardness of the moment, both subtlety wiping tears while reaching forward to click their martini glasses together. The remainder of their lunch passed without high emotion and they made plans to join together for dinner that evening. It was such a heavy lunch that Jo worried she would fall asleep in her seminar and Jill felt a compulsion to walk. Instead Jo and Jill took a taxi back to Jo's hotel. She watched out the back window to make sure no one followed them and she planned to walk from Jo's hotel to her own.

# CHAPTER 19

When she arrived back at the hotel, Nathan hadn't returned yet, so she sat down and called the detectives explaining the shooting at the cemetery.

"Are you okay Jill? None of the bullets hit you right?" said Detective Briggs.

"No I'm fine. I had a friend with me and she got a little dust in her contact lenses. The shooter nailed the marble close by, but didn't hit us. I don't know if the shooter meant to hit us or scare us – he certainly succeeded in scaring us. I'd bet your crime scene guys have more information on that. They believe the shooter was on the roof of a home across the street that was unoccupied. I expect they'll be calling you as we mentioned that we were working with you on a case."

"Yeah, while we've been talking, they reached Heyer on her cell and she's talking to them now."

"Good, I wasn't sure they believed me when I said I was working with you guys on a case."

"How did the shooter know you were going to be at the cemetery? I think we assumed that with the monster truck incident, that someone either heard your drone, or they have a camera on the field or the road. In this cemetery, they either had to have overheard you say you were going there or followed you from your hotel. How did you get there?"

"I took the St. Charles streetcar, then walked the final two to three blocks. I can't say I noticed anyone carrying a bag that would have held a rifle and wouldn't you need a rifle to hit at a distance of two hundred yards?"

"Heyer just finished her conversation, let me ask her."

There was a pause as Briggs put his phone on speaker and then she heard Heyer say, "Actually, CSI picked up three 9mm bullets at the cemetery, and three shell casings on the roof and they're matching their striations to firearms as we speak, but the initial review points to a pistol."

"So if it was a pistol, the shooter could have hid it in their clothing if they were on the streetcar with me, right?"

"Yes. It also means that the shooter is an excellent marksman and likely if he or she wanted to hit you, they could have done it," Heyer noted. "The CSI techs tested the DNA on the bullet, but there is both male and female DNA on it which you would expect from the manufacture and sales process. They're searching the home security systems in that neighborhood to see if anyone caught something on camera."

"Did you find out who owns the property that the field is on?" Jill asked completely changing the subject.

"Before we move on, I think we need to determine how someone located you at the cemetery. I can think of three ways; one - someone overheard you ask for directions to the cemetery, two – you are being followed, or three a GPS locator has been placed on you," Heyer said.

"Maybe there's a fourth method; I think hackers can follow my phone's movement through its power use."

Briggs and Heyer simultaneously said, "What?"

"Well I live close to Silicon Valley and there is always a new app to do something nefarious with. Just saying. Let me think back to my routine this morning to see if I told anyone other than Nathan that I was going to the cemetery."

Jill closed her eyes and recounted her routine that morning that took her to the cemetery. She remembered discussing it with Nathan before leaving the room. Once she left the hotel, she'd walked to the street and stood at the stop. She got on the streetcar and checked in with the conductor that she wanted off at the Lafayette Cemetery stop. The conductor told her the name of the stop and said she would announce it. So she thought about who had waited beside her at the streetcar stop and who could have heard the conversation on the street. Then she thought about who got off the streetcar at the same time and no one clicked in her mind.

The detectives waited patiently on the other end of the phone during the ensuing silence on the phone line, then Jill said, "No one sticks out in my head, but I'll admit that it could have easily happened. I'd love for my hotel room and personal stuff to be surveyed for bugs. Though if there are any in my room, they're listening to this conversation now."

"We don't have such equipment, but you can probably buy such devices online relatively cheaply."

"I might do that since I seem to run into trouble on a lot of cases. When I return to California, I'll look into equipment to detect bugs as well as ways to block my cell phone from being tracked. Meanwhile I'll check my purse to make sure no foreign objects have been placed in it and I'll begin paying attention to my surroundings to see if someone is following me. So back to my other question – who owns the land that marijuana field is planted on?"

"Interestingly, I guess you could say the State of Louisiana," replied Detective Briggs.

"Oh, is it leased to someone by the government or is the government not aware that a crop is being grown on their land?" Jill asked, the puzzlement obvious in her voice.

"Neither of those explanations and call us paranoid but this is starting to look like a big conspiracy."

"Okay now I'm really intrigued. Explain please!"

"The government owns the oceans around the United States out to twelve nautical miles. The state owns the first three miles and the federal government owns the remainder. This plot of land according to the parish tax assessor is underwater; it's part of the Gulf of Mexico."

"What? How could they be so wrong about it? Was it underwater at some point in the last fifty years or so?" Jill asked trying to comprehend how the tax assessor could be so wrong.

"I read somewhere that every forty-five minutes, a football size piece of coastal Louisiana land becomes underwater," Heyer said. "Makes you wonder if New Orleans will be here in another one-hundred years, or will it be covered by water."

"Was it just the marijuana field that was declared underwater or does it include the crops on nearby lands?" Jill asked.

"Good question, let me do some research and get back to you on that question," Heyer said.

"Regarding reclaiming land that has gone underwater, yes you can do that by taking the silt and sludge of the Mississippi and fill those wetlands in. It needs to be from the river so that it doesn't have the salt content from the gulf which prevents trees from taking root," Jill said reading from a website.

"So what does this tell us?" Briggs asked.

"It's possible that the land was underwater at some point when the original owner remanded it back to the state and then later used silt from the Mississippi River to make the land usable again. I doubt the state drives around and verifies every square mile that it owns. So this listing by the parish could be a mistake or a lack of updating to their survey maps. Maybe I'll try and pull up a survey map and see what it says as far as the water line, though really it doesn't matter how it got mislabeled and we don't know whose farming on it now."

"I guess at this point we should notify our colleagues in that parish of the location of that marijuana field and see what they do with it. If they go out and destroy it that will tell us one thing and if it's there a month from now, then that tells us something else about this case," Heyer suggested.

Another thought came to Jill and she told the detectives. "Last night Nathan and I were in a jazz club and we saw two people observing us a little more than normal. Nathan approached the one and had a conversation with him at the bar and we ended by thinking it was a mistake on our part. There was another man in the crowd who seemed to be intently observing us and so I started watching him and when he caught me watching him he took off and I didn't see him again at the club. I don't recall seeing either of those faces on the streetcar this morning. I'll start paying more attention, but Nathan and I will only be in New Orleans for another day and a half. How much trouble can we get into in that short timeline?

She heard the two detectives chuckle and Heyer said in a thick Southern voice, "Dr. Quint, I would suggest that you've experienced enough trouble for a thousand tourists and our crime statistics will decline the moment you board the plane for California."

Jill just laughed and hung up as the hotel room door opened and Nathan walked in.

CHAPTER 20

*S*he approached him to give him a welcoming kiss and a hug and asked, "How did your meeting go?"

"Good. I'm in sync with the distillery owner that's always helpful in a business relationship, and it really helped walking around the French Quarter last night. I understand what he wants to do as far as bridging the gap of typical New Orleans by having a logo that's cutting edge but includes the roots of his city. It's going to be fun to design. How was your morning? I thought you would still be out touring the Garden District."

"Jo was bored with her seminar, so she took a taxi and joined me at the Lafayette Cemetery. It was an interesting place to look at the mausoleums and then we were shot at."

Nathan's head whipped around at Jill's words, "What? Are you hurt?" He asked looking for injuries and seeing none.

"Jo and I are both fine," Jill said as she explained the situation to Nathan.

He just shook his head and pondered, "Why do these seemingly innocuous cases turn into such disasters? Seriously, you joined this case because the family said a young man died from evil spirits and that was inconsistent with your training. Now you've been chased by a monster truck and fired on with a gun while you were in a cemetery. There's just something really weird about that you being a forensic pathologist at all."

"I know what you mean. When I told Jo I could imagine that after the cemetery gates closed at night, all the dead people would come out their mausoleums to talk to each other and party, she thought I was nuts from being around dead people too much."

Nathan smiled at that thought and then he got serious and asked, "So what's your plan for the remainder of this case?"

"We got some interesting information today, but I told the detectives we were leaving in a day and a half. I can't imagine the monster truck following us home to California especially since it's not a street legal vehicle."

"So the case stays unresolved?"

"No, but I think all the evidence I could collect in this state has already been collected. Now I need to do some computer research to understand these disparate points. What does a murder by nutmeg have to do with the monster truck, a marijuana field, and the shooting in a cemetery? I'm missing something, but I don't necessarily think that identifying that something can only be done while I'm in New Orleans. What are your plans for our remaining time here?"

"I have no further meetings scheduled with my clients but there are two other distilleries I'd like to visit here just to compare what their branding principles are. Other than that I'm free to play tourist and of course I'd like to visit jazz clubs tonight and tomorrow."

"Okay, we can do all of that and more. What else would you like to see here? I didn't get my tour of the Garden District and there are a couple of museums I visited that you might enjoy, or we could leave the city completely and visit one of the plantations."

"We could go fishing."

"Really?" said Jill curiously. "I've never heard you say you like to fish."

"Fishing would not be one of my top ten activities. It just seems that we're so surrounded by water here that we should do some kind of unique water activity."

"We could rent an airboat and travel the bayous," Jill suggested.

"That sounds unique. I'm game. Do you have bug repellent with you?"

"No but there's a drug store across the street and I'll run in there and get us some stuff while you rent us an airboat."

An hour later, they approached the location of the boat rental. Jill thought she'd been brilliant for her suggestion to try the airboat. The airboat looked fun to drive, and they would see an ecosystem not found in California. The proprietor gave them a paper map as cell phone coverage inside the bayous was weak and warned them not to get lost. If they didn't come back at the appointed time, there would be a three-hundred dollar charge for their search and rescue. They were also told that a client in the past hadn't been found until the next morning. That client was sleepless and exhausted from the scare of listening to the bayou's sounds overnight. His final pitch was that if she heard sounds of snoring, it was an alligator nearby.

"I think if that man had told us one more story, I would've been too scared to take this airboat out. I'm going to be meticulous documenting where we go on this map, so we don't get lost overnight."

"Oh come on babe, it wouldn't be so bad cuddling up on this boat overnight," Nathan said with a laugh.

"Trust me, I would be eaten alive by insects and the constant scratching would keep you awake. This landscape sure is pretty out here. I love the intense greens of the trees and grasses. Some of these tree mosses look like spiderwebs. Oh look there's an alligator over there by the entrance to the swamp. I guess they're everywhere out here."

They rented an airboat that seated about six people, but it had two seats side-by-side for the driver and a passenger just how Nathan and Jill wanted to experience their trip through the bayous. The airboat was relatively quiet, as the owner had added mufflers to reduce the sound of normally loud airboats. Jill and Nathan were appreciative of the added muffler as they could carry out a conversation while driving the boat.

They had studied the map before they set out and decided to go to the furthest location first and then work their way back by exploring little avenues of each water body. It was a fun and unique adventure for the couple and they liked the lack of other airboats in the area they were exploring. So far they had passed one airboat going in the opposite direction. It appeared that the people aboard had been fishing looking at the collection of rods and fishing equipment on the boat's deck. They waved as they passed.

It was such a relaxing afternoon that Jill felt a long way from the troubles of someone shooting at her in the cemetery that morning. They had reached the farthest location of their bayou and turned the boat to begin the return trip but planned to explore the little offshoots along the way. Jill was convinced that she knew where they were as she was following the map. They were returning to the major waterway when they noticed that a boat had passed them seeming to follow their direction and touch the farthest point. But then Jill noticed something.

"I don't like the look of that boat. I see a lot of guns on that boat deck, and I don't see how you can use that quantity inside this bayou and they seem to be looking left and right in a purposeful manner."

Nathan watched for a few seconds and agreed with Jill's conclusion.

"What do you say we hightail it out of here and head back to the marina?"

"I think that's an excellent plan. Let's let that boat keep going a little farther and then we'll pull out and head back. If they don't seem to be watching, we'll stay at a slow and quiet speed. If they say something and point at us, I guess we'll find out how much horsepower is on this boat."

Jill looked around the boat for cover but there wasn't much. They could lie down in the interior of the boat, but they couldn't steer it if they did that and so they would be dead ducks.

They quietly eased out into the main waterway. Jill was looking back every few seconds, and it seemed that they were going to get away without notice. Then one of the observers on the other boat noticed them in the distance, and suddenly there was noise and action coming from the other boat as it turned headed in their direction.

"I don't suppose that's the search and rescue crew looking for us?" Jill said looking at her watch.

"I don't think so, we still have ninety minutes left on our contract. Besides why would they need guns?"

Jill nodded, glad for the boat's muffler as they took off, gaining some distance from the other boat.

"Maybe they didn't notice that we're going at a higher speed," Nathan said.

"I spoke too soon, they seem to have turned up the speed of their boat and we're no longer gaining distance on them."

"I think I'm going to have to duck into one of the small bayous after a curve in this main waterway. Can you look at the map and see if there's anything that will work for us?"

Jill studied the map and saw a body of water that might suit their needs. It wasn't a dead end, and with any luck, they might find some of that swamp moss to hide behind. She discussed the plan with Nathan and he agreed. They both knew they had no protection in the small boat.

There were a series of S-shaped curves coming up and Jill and Nathan planned to exit last in the middle of the curves. They did so and saw to their delight, a tree full of swampy moss ahead. As soon as they were on a path to the hiding place, Nathan shut off the motor, and they glided the boat into a hiding area of cypress trees and Spanish moss. She looked at the two of them clothing wise and realized they were both dressed in dark colors. Thankfully she hadn't decided to wear a red top that morning. Their boat was painted in military camouflage colors so they could sit quietly behind the moss in their seats.

Jill whispered to Nathan, "How long should we wait in here?"

"I say forty-five minutes then we start the engine at a low speed and go out the back way," he whispered in reply.

They silenced both of their cell phones and set a timer for the time span. Jill checked her cell phone coverage but showed no bars of reception. Regardless she typed a text message to the detectives and hit send with her geocoordinates in case there were a few seconds of cell tower coverage. Jill also pantomimed to Nathan that her bug repellent was the only weapon aboard their boat.

Some ten minutes later they heard the sound of a boat coming. She and Nathan tensed holding hands. They each had about a two-inch window to see through the moss. They both noted that the boat was the one that had chased them earlier. Jill thought of taking a picture, but she didn't want to move for fear of causing the smallest of waves. There were four men on the boat seated with guns of some sort strung across their chests. They could hear that the men were talking to each other, but not what they were saying over the noise of their airboat engine and fan. They continued down the waterway and about fifteen minutes later came back.

Jill and Nathan again tensed saying nothing, not moving. Still they couldn't decipher their words over the noise of the men's boat. The men didn't seem alert like they saw them and they continued on down the bayou. Once they passed again and seemed to be approaching the major waterway, Nathan looked at his watch and whispered, "We've got another twenty minutes before our arbitrary time to depart. Do you agree we should sit here for that length of time?"

"Yes, let me study this map some more. I wouldn't want to run into them in another bayou. Looks like the next two are dead-ends, although I think you can take this airboat right over a small island."

Holding up the map they agreed on the waterway that they would take to get back to the marina. They heard no further airboat traffic on the waterway in which they were hidden, and so at the appointed time moved out of their mossy hiding place and made slow progress back to the marina. Jill was keeping her fingers crossed that she'd read the map correctly and they would find their marina. Forty-five minutes later, she heaved a sigh of relief as she recognized their rental car in the parking lot of the marina. They won! They arrived safely back at the marina and had no damage to themselves or their boat.

They approached the boat owner, and Jill asked, "Did anyone show up here looking for us?"

"Yes, ma'am. They said they had emergency information for you and needed to find you. I told them approximately where I thought you might be located. Did they find you?"

"Yeah. Did you rent them a boat?"

"No they arrived with their own boat on that trailer over there," he said pointing to an SUV with a trailer.

"They must still be enjoying the swamp," Jill said.

They said their goodbyes and Jill grabbed her purse out of the trunk where they had locked it and brought it into the front seat. Nathan started the car but paused momentarily for Jill to take a few pictures of the vehicle. Then she checked her text to see if it had been sent and it was, so seeing that she had cell phone recep-tion she called the detectives in case they were planning to come to her aide.

"Jill, where are you?" Heyer asked.

"We escaped the men inside the swamp and are on our way

back to New Orleans. I just wanted to notify you in case you might be coming to our rescue and to put a stop to that."

"Are you sure you don't want an escort back to the city?"

"The men still have not come back to their trailer, so we have a good head start on them. Are you close?"

"We're about twenty minutes away from the boat rental business."

"I guess since you're part of the way out here we would appreciate the escort," Jill said giving them a description of the rental car. Then she added, "I forgot to check my purse earlier to see if it contained any tracking devices. I don't understand how they found us here without some kind of tracking device. Let me call you back as soon as I finish an examination."

"You forgot to check your purse earlier for tracking devices?" Nathan asked. "I wondered how they found us and why they couldn't find us inside the swamp. I didn't think of your purse."

Jill felt a little sheepish for forgetting the small detail and went to work searching her purse.

Two minutes later after dumping the contents out on her lap, she found what looked like a button. Knowing she had no loose buttons in her purse, she figured this was the surveillance device.

She called Heyer back and said, "Found it. Should I toss it out the window or save it for you folks?"

"There might be fingerprints on it so I would save it."

"It's too small to have fingerprints. I'll text you a picture of it."

Thirty seconds later Heyer came back on the phone and said, "Toss it out a window. I agree we won't find anything useful on it."

Jill flung it out into the waterways alongside the road they were traveling. Nathan had been monitoring his rearview mirror but saw no activity. They continued for another five minutes and saw the approaching car containing the two detectives. They stopped in the middle of the road exchanged a few words and then waited while the detectives made a U-turn and they continued back into the city.

Jill said to Nathan, "I feel like we should move our hotel as they obviously know where we have a room."

"I was thinking the same thing. Should we move to another big hotel or stay in a charming bed and breakfast?"

"Let me see if there's a hotel closer to a police station."

She did some quick research and found the hotel with the carousel bar was a block away from the French Quarter police station, and so she booked them a room. She sent the detectives' her pictures of the SUV including the VIN under the windshield. She also notified them that they were going to be moving their hotel room as soon as they got back and they liked that plan.

Nathan looked over at Jill and grinned, "Babe, it's never a dull day with you. Even a peaceful swamp cruise becomes a story to add to my memoir."

Jill had never heard of Nathan writing a memoir and asked, "Are you keeping a running list of our adventures?"

"No, I guess I should, but I wasn't planning on doing the writing for several decades. When the time comes, I'll ask to borrow your case files, and the memories will come flooding back."

She debated her response and decided to just smile smugly at him.

# CHAPTER 21

They made their hotel switch under the watchful eyes of the detectives and then walked over to their building after depositing their luggage in the new hotel room.

"We ran the plates on that vehicle and they came back as belonging to a corporation that we've been unable to trace. Likewise the VIN."

"Has it come up before in your vehicle searches?" Nathan asked curiously. Mostly he was silent during Jill's investigations as it was far from his area of expertise, but the occasional question popped out.

"Yes, on a rare occasion. Usually, it's because someone's re-engineered the VIN and they have stolen plates. This time the plates are not stolen, but the company that owns them seems to be nonexistent," replied Heyer.

"I wonder if it's that same company that owns land near the marijuana field. Let me search through my emails from my friend Jo Pringle. I'm sure she mentioned the name of the company. Nathan and I are supposed to meet her for dinner in a couple of hours, and I'll see if she's found any more information on the company she was searching for which may be the one that owns the vehicle that followed us to the marina. I also have two other team members that I might call on for additional information. One of them is a social media maven and perhaps, she'll find information about the company."

Jill found the email from Jo and compared the name to the one of the car registration, but it was different.

"The companies are different, rats! Tell me how does car registration work in Louisiana. Do you have to provide a social security number? Do corporations have to provide any special kind of identification since they wouldn't have a social security number?"

"Yes, they have to submit an employer tax paying ID number. I'll check with the Internal Revenue Service and see if they can find a reason for the discrepancy," Heyer said. "I doubt I'll have an answer for a few days."

Jill couldn't think of anything else to say about the case and so said, "Detectives, this might be our last face to face meeting as Nathan and I return to California tomorrow. I'll keep working on this case remotely from California until it gets solved or I pick up a new case of my own. I'll keep you posted if any of my team members find out anything new about these two mysterious companies."

The detectives stood up and they shook hands adding, "I'm surprised to say that it's been a pleasure to work with you. I'm surprised because I thought at best you'd be in our way, and at worst you would contaminate a crime scene and harm our case, but you made the discovery that this was a homicide and you've contributed to our evidence and you've attracted what we presume is the killer which further confirms that something big is going on behind this homicide."

Jill and Nathan said their goodbyes and were shortly out on the street window shopping. They had another three hours before they were meeting Jo for dinner. So they visited a few distilleries so Nathan could get a feel for his new client's competition. While they sipped rum at the first distillery, Jill sent a summary email to Angela and Marie bringing them up to speed on the case with a request that they investigate the two mysterious companies if they had time over the next few days; Marie through social media, and Angela connecting photos to them.

They joined Jo for dinner at a fantastic seafood restaurant in the area west of the French Quarter. They started with grilled chicken in a white BBQ sauce and fish sticks in beer batter. They moved on to main courses of smothered catfish, jumbo shrimp, and grilled tuna with sides of creamed corn, fried brussels sprouts, and white beans and bacon. Jo and Nathan were adventurous with their food choices while Jill was conservative. Still, they shared their fish entrees confirming for Jill that she still didn't like shrimp or catfish no matter who the chef was.

They lingered, wanting dessert, but needing some time to digest the excellent meal. If dessert was anything like the main courses, they were in for a scrumptious time.

"How was the seminar this afternoon? Less boring than the morning?"

"Well nobody shot at me in the ballroom, so yes it was rather tame!" Jo said with a grin. "The discussion was more interesting as it was an analysis of the recent tax bill's impact on our business and some strategies to mitigate or take advantage of those changes."

"Personally, I think I'd rather dodge bullets than listen to that topic. Kudos to you for finding it interesting," Nathan said.

"You two would find the topic interesting if all of a sudden the government applied a creativity tax to every product you created Nathan and an alcohol abuse education tax for every liter of wine you produce."

"Ouch," said Jill and Nathan simultaneously.

"Personally, I'd be out of business probably as I don't produce enough wine to offset a new expense."

"Exactly why I find the topic interesting. It appeals to my

financial mind to figure out how to minimize the tax and maximize the deductions related to any new legislation."

"On that terrifying scenario of new taxes, did you find out anything new about that corporation that we've been unable to identify or the new one I forwarded you the name of today."

"As a matter of fact, I did. In between strategizing tax policies, I was running through the Paradise Papers to get a sense of the secret world of tax havens in hopes of finding our company there. The company was good, but I'm better. The company's incorporation and name changes moved from the Caymans to Hong Kong, and on to Switzerland which are all highly secret countries. Did you know there are one-hundred-forty-seven international banks on that tiny island of about fifty-thousand people?"

"So did you figure it out?" Jill asked following Jo's incorporation journey around the world.

"Of course, but once I tell you, you'll want to call your detective friends and high tail it out of this state so let's have dessert first."

"And of course you've known of this problem for a few hours and felt no need to tell the story until dessert," Nathan said with a grin. "I like your kicked-back attitude about the investigation."

"A girl has got to have her priorities; besides helping Jill with her detective cases, I admit on occasion, I'll put a great meal and an excellent dessert before my contributions to a case."

"I'll keep that in mind," said Jill pretending sangfroid. Then she leaned forward and whispered urgently, "Spill the beans, who or what is this corporation?"

"Seriously Jill, I won't say anything inside this restaurant as we don't know who's listening and this corporation ratcheted-up the stakes this morning with the rifle shots. Of course that's assuming they're behind it, but until I know otherwise, it's safer to assume they're at the root of it."

"Then let's leave now," Jill said wanting to know Jo's information.

"Jill, thirty minutes won't make a difference in the scheme of things. You're just going to have to wait until I finish my salted caramel cake."

"Com'on Jill, when have you turned down key lime pie?" Nathan asked. "Besides I want to try their magic cake. Let's have patience and finish our meal. You have the rest of the evening to hear Jo's news."

Jill heaved a sigh and surrendered to their wishes. She felt the urge to gobble her dessert both because it was delicious and she wanted to hear Jo's news, but she'd never been good at fast eating. Jo on the other hand had been raised in a large family and experience had taught her to eat fast or lose out. She knew she could always count on Jo to clean her plate quickly.

Finally, they finished their dessert, settled the bill, and made to depart the restaurant. Nathan paused at the door and asked Jill and Jo, "Do we walk or call a car service?"

Jo replied, "Normally, I'd say, let's walk, but tonight, given today's incident at the cemetery, we should call a car service to take us. In fact, I'm so paranoid, I would say we should split up and take two or three separate cars."

Jill's eyes went bug-eyed with thoughts of who the mysterious client was. It really had Jo rattled. She said, "Okay, how about if you and I take one car and Nathan can take another. We'll have the restaurant call a taxi company and we'll use my car service app. That should be as random as we can make it."

They did as planned with Nathan's taxi showing up before their car service, but they could see the car in the distance heading their way and so they convinced Nathan to get into his car.

Less than a minute later, Jo and Jill were getting into the back seat of a silver SUV. As the drive was so short, Jill had sweetened the pot with the promise of a ten dollar tip. Once she did their car was routed their way and they left for the short journey to Jo's hotel. When they got there, they found Nathan waiting for them. They decided to have their discussion in the hotel's exercise room figuring there wouldn't be many customers at this time of the night and they lucked out as there were none.

"Okay I find all this secrecy to be weird. Who's the person behind the corporation that has you so spooked?" Jill asked.

"I won't bore you with the chain of documents I ran through until I reached the end, but the person that owns that marijuana field is the husband of United States Senator Stephanie Harris."

"Really?" Jill said, turning that information over in her mind. "Why are you so convinced that she represents a clear and present danger?"

"Because there were so many deceptions in the incorporation documents. I had to hunt through countless documents and I can't remember how many incorporations to find the owner and guess what? He's dead. Why would a single pot field need that much secrecy? There's something more there. Perhaps Marie can check her sources."

"I asked for her and Angela's help earlier and I'll forward this name to them. What do you mean he's dead?"

"The senator was married just after college and her husband died in a car accident over twenty years ago. The document listing him as the owner was filed in the last year. That's a very long time to be using your dead husband's name especially since you remarried and had kids with another man before divorcing him. His last name is not Harris, it's Carter and I spent a long time figuring out how he was related. I'm heading home early tomorrow morning and I can't wait to get out of town. No offense Nathan and Jill, but this case is becoming hot, and I don't want to be attached to it."

"This is turning out to have more layers than I thought when I took this case on. Even when Alicia and I determined that this was a homicide by nutmeg, I thought I just had a smart murderer, perhaps there was an angry woman in his background since nutmeg poisoning would point to that. I didn't think I'd have an angry female senator. Do you have the documents or the steps that you went through to arrive at your conclusion? I'll need to recreate it for the detectives. They would blow me off without evidence."

"I'll spend some time creating a flow chart for you tonight and I'll email it to you."

"Do you feel safe in your hotel room," Nathan asked. "I could get us a suite at my hotel or perhaps one here that we can share."

"As Jill said I'm overly spooked and after I email you the flow chart, I'm sure I'll crash into sleep after that wonderful dinner and the tedious work of documenting my research. I'll be fine."

"Okay then, do me a favor and put together your flowchart in the business center of the hotel. That way if there's anyone watching our departure from this hotel with plans to search your hotel room, they will find it empty," Nathan said.

"Okay now you're scaring me with the offer of the joint room and suggesting I work in the business center."

"We're both scaring each other with our thoughts," Nathan acknowledged. "You have our cell phones, call us if you need us."

"Will do and I do like your idea of the business center," Jo said giving Jill and Nathan goodbye hugs. "I don't know when I'll see you guys again, but I'm sure it won't be long before you try to get us involved in a new case."

"Always looking to pad our vacation fund," Jill said in reply and they walked to the business center and left Jo inside and exited the hotel.

"Do you think she's safe there alone?" Jill asked Nathan.

"It depends."

"On what?"

"If she's been associated with you and this case, then I don't think she's safe. If you're the sole target, then she's safer by herself than with us."

"That's my thinking. I'm going to hope there was no way to identify who the person was who was with me in the cemetery and no attacks have been made on Alicia."

They left the hotel and walked the two blocks to their own

hotel without incident. Nathan said to Jill, "I really should have checked with you before I booked this hotel. If I had I would have booked us into her hotel."

"Not to worry. After you booked into this hotel, I looked into moving us to Jo's hotel, but it sold out with the convention she's attending."

They settled in to do work, Nathan playing with some design sketches for his new client and Jill checking in with Angela and Marie to see if they would have time to contribute to the case. Then she saw the email come through from Jo on her investigation. She was reading the email when her cell phone rang.

Surprised that anyone would be calling her at this late hour, she was immediately worried. Checking the caller ID, she saw it was Jo. She said to Nathan as she hit the connect button, "It's Jo."

"Hey Jo, what's up? I was just going over your email."

"I just returned to my room and someone's ransacked it and I can't stay here. Can you send Nathan to come get me?"

"We're on our way. Where are you now?"

"I closed the door and returned to the lobby. Wasn't sure if I should call hotel security or if you should call your detective friends."

"I'm going to have Nathan connect with you on his cell so I can free up mine to call the detectives. Hang up on me when you see his incoming call."

Seconds later she heard Nathan connecting and they were almost at Jo's hotel. She fished through her purse for the detective's card and dialed Heyer's number. It was after hours and she wasn't sure either detective would take her call.

"Yes, Jill?"

"Hello detective. I'm on my way to the hotel my friend was staying at who was in the cemetery with me today. Her room has been ransacked and I think it has something to do with our case. Would you like me to call hotel security or will the New Orleans police handle this?"

"We will. Is she hurt? Did she see the suspects?"

"Thanks, no and no. She found some interesting information today for the case and she was in the business center compiling it and found the mess when she got to her room. She immediately closed the door and returned to the lobby and called me. I suppose for all we know, the suspect is still in her hotel room."

"When you get to the hotel stay in the lobby with your friend. Do not enter the room. I'll be there in ten minutes and I'll see if Briggs is available. Understand?"

"Yes," and she heard the click of the phone call ending just as they were walking into the lobby of Jo's hotel. She was seated in a lobby chair, eyes closed fingers together and raised upward like she was meditating, or perhaps she was just asleep. Then Jill saw that she had her cell phone cradled under her jaw, so no peaceful meditation going on there. Jill hurried over to give her friend a hug. Nathan went to work arranging for a different hotel room that would accommodate the three of them while Jill notified Jo of the police's pending arrival.

"Thank goodness you backed out of the room. What if the intruder was still in your hotel room?"

"I didn't even think of that! I just know from working with you on these cases to try and not contaminate the scene and fortunately I was alert enough to think of that. I don't know if anything was missing. By good luck, I had my purse, iPad, and cellphone with me. The only thing an intruder could have stolen was my clothes or some inexpensive hair products."

"I'm just glad you're safe. It was one of the first things the detective asked and then she told me to stay in the lobby with you until she arrives. We could go over to the hotel bar and have a drink while we wait for her, it'll be another five to ten minutes."

"I'm fine, Nathan had me breathing deep on his way over here and that went a long way to calming me down. If I haven't said this before, you're lucky to have him."

"Okay then let's sit here and wait for the detective. Nathan's making arrangements to move us to a two queen room or a suite so that we'll be in the same space."

"Sounds like a plan. I'm thinking we're not going to get much sleep tonight by the time we're done with our explanations for the detectives and moving across town. Maybe we can sleep in in the morning. What time is your flight?"

"We're leaving at two, and you?"

"I'm leaving at four. I'll just travel with you guys to the airport and hang out there. I have to think the bad guys can't get to me beyond security," Jo said with a small smile.

"Maybe the detective can hook you up with some additional airport security or maybe they'll want to hear your explanation about the senator during that time."

"I hope not. I'd rather the police issue a bulletin saying I'm a worthless witness," Jo said with a tired grin. "It's the first time in my life I'm asking to be called stupid. I don't want trouble following me home to Green Bay. Jack would not appreciate criminals following me home from one of your cases."

Jack was Jo's partner and he was always concerned about Jo's well-being, but never more so when she got involved in one of Jill's cases.

"Let's see what we can convince them to do. I have your email and so I think I've got a good grasp on your research. It's a lot farther to follow me home to California for those involved in this case."

## CHAPTER 22

*J*ill was sitting with Jo and the two of them watched Detective Heyer stride across the hotel lobby toward them. She was wearing jeans with her detective shield affixed to the waist holding a cell phone in one hand.

In short order, the detective had Jo's name and contact information and they went upstairs to her room. Lobby staff had noted the detective's arrival and they soon had a hotel security guard trailing along after them.

The detective had Jo open her door, then she stated in a loud voice, "This is the New Orleans Police entering the room." The detective entered with her gun in front of her and a patrol officer covering her back. They quickly determined there was no human in the room. They were told not to touch anything. A crime scene tech arrived to collect evidence from the room.

Jo looked intently at her belongings trying to determine what was missing and said, "I don't believe anything's missing. I mean I haven't counted my undies or my makeup products, but it looks like everything is here."

"No technology? Laptop?" Heyer asked.

"No I travel with my iPad and I had it with me in the business center and at dinner. That's the value of carrying a big purse," Jo said with a strained smile.

The crime scene tech had taken Jo's fingerprints so she could be eliminated from anything they found. As it was a hotel room it was likely containing lots of DNA and fingerprints. The tech concentrated on the interior zipper tabs of Jo's luggage as that was the one area outside of TSA agents, that would likely contain only her fingerprints. In short order, Jo had her bags packed and was ready to move over to Nathan and Jill's hotel. Nathan had lucked out by finding a hotel room with a connecting door. Jo would feel secure if she knew they were close by.

"Ms. Pringle, I would like to hear about the research you did related to the marijuana field that Dr. Quint identified," Heyer requested. She was on her own with this part of the investigation as Briggs was out of the area.

Earlier Jill and thought that Jo was overreacting with her paranoia about the conversation on the marijuana field ownership. Now that she's seen the damage to Jo's room she likewise was worried about who could hear their conversation. She said to Heyer, "Can we have this conversation in your car? Jo here was paranoid earlier about who would overhear her describe her research and she was right to feel that way. I'm afraid our own room at our hotel may not be secure. When Jo called us, Nathan and I hurried over to her and we brought our own technology with us in case we would be targeted next. So we have everything we need for this conversation."

Heyer thought about the situation and the fact that her own car had sat under the hotel's porte-cochère. She'd never seen anything like this in prior cases, so maybe it would pay off for her to take the group somewhere private and not predictable. She had a cousin that ran a jazz club and Heyer had been in her office and knew it was large enough to accommodate the four of them. With the music outside of the office, they wouldn't have to worry about eavesdroppers.

"Let's go in my car. I know a quiet place where we can talk."

They piled into her sedan car and watched her navigate the New Orleans streets.

Jill engaged Nathan in a conversation about the bottle labels they had seen at the rum distillery. If the detective's car was bugged and someone was listening, they would be irked by the nonessential conversation. The detective parked the car and they walked three blocks and to Nathan's pleasant surprise, walked into a jazz club. The detective made her way to the bar and asked the bartender something. He gestured that she proceed to the right side back and they did so.

Heyer had them wait in the space outside of a closed-door and she entered the room.

Jill, Jo, and Nathan looked at each other puzzled by the detective's choice. Nathan shrugged and said, "The music is good here, I wouldn't mind staying and listening to it. Maybe I'll take a seat at the bar, enjoy the music, and protect your backs in case anyone should head for this doorway."

Jill and Jo nodded thinking that was a reasonable idea. Nathan hadn't been involved in the search for the marijuana field's owner and could contribute nothing to the conversation other than supporting the two of them. He deserved some musical enjoyment and he would indeed protect their backs.

Heyer came back out with another woman. The detective introduced her as a cousin and said that she'd given them the use of her office for their conversation. Nathan described his own plans and followed the cousin to the bar. Soon the three women were seated in the office. It was plain with a desk and three chairs. The desk was littered with a computer screen, schedules, and bills from what they could see as the Detective took a seat behind the desk while Jill and Jo were seated in the guest chairs.

"I think you'll agree that our conversation should be secure in this office. My car might have been bugged, your hotel room might've been bugged, but there's no way that anyone could've gotten ahead of us tonight and bugged this office."

"It's a brilliant location Detective and as an added bonus, Nathan will get to enjoy the music he loves while watching to make sure no one gets close to this office. He's a master black belt in hapkido and could put a thug on their back in no time."

"I'll admit, I felt kind of stupid with all this cloak and dagger stuff for a threat that I am in no way sure is real, but I also understand that our department never thought despite the shooting at the cemetery, that you were under any risk from an unknown entity. We were wrong, so perhaps a little paranoia on my part will keep us all alive."

Jo and Jill relaxed with that explanation. It was one thing to be under threat, and it was another thing not to be believed.

"So Ms. Pringle tell me a little about yourself. How do you know Dr. Quint and what do you usually do on the cases that she takes on. Then I'd like an explanation of what you looked for in her current case."

"It's late at night and I'm a little tired from my normal day and the added stress of these two attacks on me. We'll just use first names here? I'm Jo. She's Jill, and you are?"

"Julie."

"Thank you. Now onto your question about my background Julie. I'm a CPA and by day, I do financial work. When Jill pulls me into a case, I become a forensic accountant. No, I'm not certified in that, but I'm damn good. In fact, my work is probably responsible for finding at least half of Jill's criminals. Would you agree, Jill?"

"Yes I would!"

"Okay. When Jill takes on a case, she usually drops an email to me and two other friends as we all help her on these cases. Often times there isn't a defined role for any of us at the start of the case. It's simply an FYI notification and as facts begin to accumulate in a case she brings in one or more of us to help. In this case you got my services for free because I happen to be here in New Orleans for a financial seminar and I had spare time and an easy location to devote to this case. Jill gave me the coordinates of the various farms around her victim's field sampling that was suspicious. As a routine matter, I search for financial information of the people connected to a case. I looked at the ownership of those farms. While in most cases farms are privately held, you'd be amazed at the information you can gather about them."

"Do you have a diagram or something that describes how you arrived at your sources of information?" Heyer asked.

"It's all in the email that I sent to Jill."

"I appreciate that you laid it out in an email, but I would be remiss as a detective if I didn't ask you for a firsthand account of it."

Jo went on to describe the trail she'd followed while the detective furiously took notes asking questions now and again. At times, Jill thought the detective wanted to jump ahead and ask who was the owner, but she would restrain herself knowing that she was getting a lesson in financial detecting. When Jo delivered the shocking conclusion of ownership, Heyer looked extremely uneasy. She followed and agreed with Jo's every step in her research, but she didn't like the conclusion as it would make her life as a police officer oh so complicated and risky. There was a long history of state and local officials charged and convicted of various illegal acts almost all of them for money she recalled. She could even remember a few cases in which the political figure hired hit men to target a witness or jury member.

"I've followed your explanation and I'm taking notes and I'll have your email, and despite all of the crooked criminals we have in the history of Louisiana, I'm still shocked at this one. I'll do the research on the senator but I believe one of her platforms year in and year out is to block marijuana from being legalized in Louisiana."

"From a financial analysis perspective, I have to say her

behavior makes a lot of sense. If marijuana is legalized, then every farmer can grow it and I know that some states like California have worried that crops like lettuce and strawberries would be given up to plant marijuana. If marijuana is illegal, then it's harder to get, and its price goes up because you can't buy it at just any supermarket on the street. If I wanted to maximize my profit as a marijuana dealer I would want it to be illegal in this state and for me to have a way to grow it in secret which is what I think you have here. I wonder how many other corn stocks are hiding other crops of marijuana. Perhaps she owns a company that grows pot legally in one of the legalized states, and she exports it to Louisiana because she has a seller network set up here."

"I see," said the detective mulling over things in her head about the situation and her next steps. She took a look at her watch and realized it was getting very late. The jazz club probably had already issued the last call. While it was legal to serve alcohol twenty-four hours a day in New Orleans, a jazz club typically made the last call shortly before they closed for the night.

"I'm going to work on this case and I may need to consult with you at times. You're both an expert on how to maximize financial gain, and you're also the sharpest forensic accountant who is not certified that I've ever met. I would appreciate once you returned home that you remain available by phone or email to answer my questions," Heyer said looking directly at Jo.

"Of course I'll be available. Maybe not at the moment you call if I'm in a business meeting, but I'll return your call as soon as possible."

"Is email a better way to contact you?"

Jo laughed and said, "No, I'm drowning in email and have at any given time, a thousand unread emails. Just leave me a message on my cell phone and I'll get back to you. I'll likely have little time to do more work for you, but if you have a few days before you need answers, I might be able to help."

They wrapped up the meeting and left the office to find Nathan nearly alone at the bar talking to Heyer's cousin.

"We're ready to head back to our hotel. I'm not sure where we are in relation to our hotel, Detective. Are we within walking distance?"

"It's a little far to walk – about eight blocks given that an unknown source may want to take aim at you, and you folks are tired I know. Why don't I drop you off?"

They agreed and piled into her car. Thirty minutes later, Jo had settled into her new hotel room, and Jill and Nathan had retired as well.

"How was the jazz in the club," Jill asked.

"It was very enjoyable and the club owner was great to talk to as well. We had a lot of favorite jazz musicians in common that we discussed and a few had played at her place. Pretty cool."

"I noticed she had a drawing in front of her. Did you do that for her?"

"Yeah. She asked me what I did and I told her. She then said that as long as I was standing around, could I create a logo for her brand? It was a challenge I couldn't resist as she was sure I couldn't do it and she doubted that being a wine label designer was my real job."

"Really?" Jill let out a laugh. "I wish I had been there to watch that interaction. Was she pleased with what you designed for her?"

"Yeah, she was. Of course, it's on a cocktail napkin so she'll need some help to transfer the image into usable materials, but that's okay. I won at the end of the night."

"Sorry honey, but I think she won. She conned one of the most famous label artists in the world for a free design."

"Oh well, it was an amusing way to pass the evening," Nathan said curling into her at the end of a very long day.

# CHAPTER 23

The next morning the three friends checked out of their hotel and went out for a late breakfast prior to heading to the airport. Jill was in a quandary as to whether to recommend a French café or the famous Café Du Monde. She settled for the café as it was smaller and quieter and they had so many great things on their menu. At least they would be able to watch who entered and tried to get too close. The Café Du Monde was so large that it would be difficult to scout everyone in the area. It would be a risky locale. Nathan and Jo really enjoyed the items they ordered off the menu. Alicia had been able to join them for their final New Orleans meal and enjoyed hearing about their adventures of the last few days. From there they had a short walk back to the hotel and a car service would take them to the airport. Once they were through security, they thought they would be able to relax.

"I wonder how they identified me and my location?" Jo mused. "You, they caught surveying their soybean field with your drone, but I could have been a random person exploring the same area of the cemetery as you."

"Maybe they used facial recognition software to identify you.

Who knows if the guy or gal that shot at us, took our picture first," Jill suggested.

"Does the average person have access to that kind of software?"

"Yes. I debated buying a program for my business, but decided it wouldn't get used enough to justify the expense."

"Okay maybe the answer as to how they found me doesn't add to this case."

"It'll be interesting to see what the cops do with this case. There are some unknowns here that they should research before they acknowledge publicly that they're working on the case."

"Yeah, my first order of business would be to try and find how many plots of land this senator owns. Then I'd want to know how many of those plots are growing marijuana, and how many are grown on state property as it's alleged to be underwater," Jo said. "This politician really irks me so the police need to arrest her and end her empire. She grows pot illegally on land that she doesn't own since she's arranged for the tax rolls to say it belongs to the state, and the hypocrite votes down any resolution that eases the regulations around pot."

"Tell us what you really think!" Nathan said. He'd been sitting, people watching, and doodling while the two women talked.

"How would you go about doing that?" Jill asked, with a smile for Nathan's comment. She had some ideas but she wanted to hear what Jo had to say to see if she was on target.

"I suppose there's some satellite that the police could check with and view lands around Louisiana. It might take time to get the video footage they need. For something faster, I'd rent a small plane and a videographer, and fly the entire southern coast of Louisiana. I think there's a second set of properties that might be away from the Gulf and for those, I would do a computer search of property ownership by all those false names that she used for the first acre that we discovered. That would wrap up the properties she owns. Next I would go after her distribution network, and

I'm sure the cops have a way of tracking narcotics, so I would leave it to them. I might call in the FBI to actually press charges given some of the problems with bribed judges in the state. I think one of their areas of expertise is public corruption. This is a risky case for the cops as someone in the senator's organization knows that someone is investigating a piece of her business. Unless the New Orleans police can bring some consultants into this case, our two detective friends are going to be months collecting the information. Maybe that's also the reason to call the FBI -just to get additional resources to help them on the case."

"After I get back to California, I'll give Marie and Angela a call to see if they have any ideas on how to speed up the collection of evidence for the detectives. Between Marie's expertise at ferreting out information on individuals and Angela's knowledge about photography, maybe they'll have some suggestions on how to speed up the investigation."

"Yeah, we need to speed it up. I'm afraid these criminals are going to follow me back to Green Bay and take some shots there. Maybe I'll give the detectives a call right now, and ask them to call the Green Bay Police and the Brown County Sheriff to see if I can get some added protection. Call me paranoid, but there's an evil enterprise behind the senator."

"Jo, I think that's an excellent idea and I'll have them call my Sheriff as well. He won't appreciate the call given the damage my first big case caused to his headquarters, but it's not our fault we're just doing our job for the family of Mr. Cheval."

"It's good to be reminded of his name, sometimes these cases of yours get so complex and take on a life of their own, that I forget that they always start with some poor murdered victim who is often unaware of some bigger situation that they accidentally touched and it got them killed."

"Yeah," Jill agreed quietly. Poor Mr. Cheval never knew what hit him, just that he had felt ill in the month before his death, but he never had the opportunity to understand why he felt so sick.

"Well ladies, you've wrapped up a conversation about the case and now you're drifting into morose thoughts. How about a happier conversation? Have you planned your next vacation yet? Is the location near any wineries, so that I can join you at the very end of your trip and learn about a new wine region in the world?"

"Actually I haven't had a chance to talk to Jill about a location, but a few weeks ago, Angela, Marie, and I were discussing where to go on our next vacation over drinks. We were thinking about Canada- maybe Toronto, Montréal, and Québec city. What do you think of the idea, Jill?"

"I haven't been to Toronto for a while. As a child, we used to vacation there because that's where my mom's relatives are from. I've never been to Montréal or Québec city, so I think that's an excellent suggestion. Were you thinking of the spring of next year?"

"We hadn't talked about specific dates, but the spring would work for me. Nathan, is there wine in that part of the world?"

"Like Wisconsin, there are some wineries in Canada, I believe in the area near Niagara Falls. However, somewhere in that area, they are producing ice wines which I would love to explore. So that location works for me!"

"Then we're set! Canada it is!" Jo said.

Jill had taken a moment to call the detectives and request that they call their respective law enforcement agencies in California and Wisconsin to notify them of potential activity related to the case once the women returned home. Then Jill and Nathan's flight was called for boarding, and they stood up and hugged and said their goodbyes. Later they all arrived back at their homes and had received messages from their local law enforcement to call them in the morning.

# CHAPTER 24

The next morning, Jill and Trixie went for their run along the country roads surrounding Jill's vineyard. Even though it was October, in California's Central Valley the day would be in the low nineties later. On her to do list, was to call the sheriff, once she was out of the shower after her run. She and Nathan had taken one of the last flights to the West Coast, and she had a few more hours, she was sure before any of the Senator's people could arrive in her community. Sure they could've arrived late at night to Los Angeles and rented a car to drive north overnight, but she doubted they were that fast-moving. Also on her list of things, was to check the health of her grapevines, and check the sales of her most recent vintage at her local wine stores. This was her third vintage, and the first two had sold out within a month of release. This year she had doubled her production to twelve thousand bottles of Moscato and now she worried about selling them all. She debated holding back 500 bottles to sell online, but when she looked at the regulations of selling an alcohol product she decided against it. Now she was looking for an online broker to take care of it for her and so she would spend sometime later that day making calls.

She also made appointments with Marie and Angela to discuss the case by phone with them. She was hopeful that information they could source would greatly speed up the collection of evidence for the case. She hoped that the Senator's organization would focus their energy on law enforcement rather than the four of them.

An hour later, she was showered and heading into town to meet with Sheriff Arstand. Ever since his station had been shot up by a prior bad group of criminals, he always looked like he had indigestion when he met Jill face-to-face.

She walked into his office and held out her hand to shake with the sheriff and said, "Hello Sheriff, I understand that Detectives Briggs and Heyer briefed you yesterday about the case I got involved with in New Orleans."

"Yes Dr. Quint, I spoke with them. Let me know when you plan to retire permanently as a forensic pathologist. My department will fund your retirement party. We'll be able to do that on the savings we'll get for not having to protect you anymore."

"Com'on Sheriff! Look at my protection as training for your department. I'm sure it's one of the many reasons Deputy Davis keeps up her sharpshooter skills."

"All kidding aside, it looks like you've landed yourself in another mess with this case. Your political corruption cases seem to turn more violent, than your garden-variety crooks that you uncover. I understand that you were shot at in a cemetery, intimidated by a monster truck, chased by an airboat in a swamp, and your friend's hotel room was searched. Does that cover your situation?"

"Yes sir. It's been quiet this morning, but then I figured it would take the bad guys a while to get to the West Coast and the Palisades Valley so I think I'm safe until this evening if they followed my trail."

"I suspect they will. Three attempts on you and your friend

means they're serious about ending your role in the investigation. Those two detectives had better watch their backs too."

"We suggested that they bring the FBI into the case as there's political corruption involved and that's an area of their expertise. Also Louisiana has a long history of corrupt public officials including judges and I have to think that this Senator has her tentacles into all kinds of places to make life difficult for those detectives to go anywhere with this case."

"That's not good to hear. I think I'll call our local FBI office to bring them up to speed on the case and have them on standby in case we should need their help protecting you in the Palisades Valley."

"Thank you Sheriff. I worry about my friends that are also working on this case in Green Bay. Do you think you could call your colleagues there and reinforce the seriousness of the bad people that I've stirred up and what they might expect?"

"Yes I'll do that, but you might also make the call. As I recall you had a prior case in Green Bay that followed you home to the Palisades Valley that they were involved in. It wouldn't hurt to refresh their memory about that case from your perspective. Do you have the contact information of the officers involved?"

"I do. I've got computerized records backed up to the cloud of every case I've ever handled including the names, badge numbers and telephone numbers of every law enforcement person I've worked with. I'll contact them - that was good advice, thank you."

"On our end, we'll increase patrols toward your property, looking for suspicious behavior. Given that there are wineries in the area, we have no way of watching for strangers. You've got a good security system on your house if I recall, and sadly that may be our first indication of trouble."

"I'd have to agree with your conclusions, Sheriff. Is Deputy Davis on duty this month?"

"She is. She took a vacation last month; if trouble occurs while she is on duty, she'll be locked and loaded and ready to protect."

They concluded their meeting and Jill left the station. She stopped at the grocery store to supply her refrigerator after the seven day absence. She spoke with Nathan on the way home to relay the conversation with the Sheriff and he couldn't think of anything to add to what they were planning to do. They made plans for dinner at his house that evening and ended the call. Jill had just enough time to unload her groceries before her call with Marie.

"How's it going? Your email sounded very eventful! I bet the airboat chase was scary in the middle of a swamp."

"Yeah! What started as a fee-free case of death by evil spirits for an old classmate has turned into a political corruption case with a Senator who has a whole lot to lose. I just had a meeting with Sheriff Arstand and I'm going to call the detectives in your city that we worked with during the case where a physician was killed on the second hole green. I have Detectives Van Bruggin and Haro listed in my notes. Does that sound familiar?"

"I wouldn't remember their names, so I would go with your notes and I think that's a great idea to give them a call."

"So the thing we need help with is identifying all the pieces of land belonging to the senator that are growing pot. And of those growing pot, which plots are considered underwater and therefore owned by the state of Louisiana. Can you think of a quick way to figure that out? I seek not only to help the detectives in New Orleans but because I think that until the case is made public with the evidence presented perhaps in a major newspaper or TV station, then Jo and I will remain under threat from the Senator's people. If the word gets out to the public, then harming us won't derail the case."

"I have some ideas of where I might find that information. I have an office meeting in about thirty minutes; it will take another half hour, and then I can leave the office early and work on your case the rest of today. With any luck, I'll have a way to collect the information you're looking for by this evening! By the way does underwater mean literally under the water of the Gulf of Mexico?"

"Yes, Louisiana is losing a lot of land every year to the Gulf. Thanks for having a plan. Keep me posted. Oh and by the way I heard we're going to Canada in the spring?"

"Did Jo mention that? I'm glad you like the choice. It looked like there was a lot to do and it's close by - no twelve hour flight to get there and six time zones to conquer."

"You have my vote and Nathan's. Of course he's not coming with us, rather he'll join us at the end. He mentioned there are a lot of ice wines in that part of Canada."

They said their goodbyes and ended the call. Jill checked her watch and it was nearly time to speak with Angela. Time to refresh her drink and then talk on the phone again.

"Hey girlfriend, how are you doing?" Jill asked.

"Better than you from the sounds of your email. I'm surprised Jo was willing to get involved with this case. She made a few comments in Scotland on the last case that made me think she was going to decide not to help anymore."

"I thought so too and was surprised when she offered to help. At one point during our time in New Orleans she offered the explanation that we did really honorable work helping victims find justice. She didn't like that our lives were put at risk, but she saw the importance of the work, so I think she's fully committed and back on the team thankfully. I don't know what I'd do without her as a resource. In so many cases financial dealings point to the culprit. I really need her help. Indeed I really need all of my friends' help. You each have skills that make the cases go faster. I think that's often why we can solve faster than law enforcement, it's our diverse menu of skills in our small team. But enough of that self-congratulatory behavior. I was hoping to enlist your help in the case."

"I'm here to help and despite some of the violent people that we come into contact with on these cases, I enjoy using my professional resources to help. You're asking me at a good time. I'm past school photos, and not quite ramping up for holiday pictures. What do you need?"

"We're trying to come up with a list of properties that grow pot on them and we need Geo-coordinates for those farm plots. I do say this sounds weird because I live in a state where it's not illegal to grow pot and I'm chasing down a politician that grows pot. Weird huh?"

"That's not what bothers you about this case. You're mad because someone is killing or attempting to kill people who know of those pot fields. That's where they crossed the line."

"True."

"So you would like me to find pictures of fields in Louisiana that are growing pot and somehow connect those pictures to Geo-coordinates. Right? I can do that."

"How?"

"There's software that will guess at the location. I just need to find the pictures. It would go much faster and be more accurate if you sent me up in a plane to snap pictures of the coast."

"That's what Jo suggested, but there are 380 miles of the coast. Small airplanes fly from 100 to 150 mph, and because the shape of the coastline is jagged you might have to make at least two passes. So I would guess that would be about eight hours of video footage that you would have to slow down to look at and see if there were any marijuana plants down below. If you could find information that already exists, that would be much faster."

"I'll look around for some satellite images and check the National Hurricane Center. They take a lot of images from space that might be useful. Okay now I'm going to check a bunch of websites and see what I can find overall, then I'll drop you an email and tell you what my timeline is likely to be to get you the information you're looking for, and then you can decide if you would rather send me up in a small airplane," Angela said humorously.

"Sounds like a plan. Let's try the low-budget method today. If it appears that there aren't good images available, we will move on to trying you out in an airplane!"

They finished their conversation including a few comments about the future vacation in Canada. Once Jill was done with her phone calls, she decided it was time to check out her house security system. It was true, that it was sophisticated and she had it installed on one of her first big cases when someone was trying to murder her. Since that time her diligence in turning the system on left a lot to be desired. Now she'd make sure it was on. Then she had an idea.

# CHAPTER 25

Jill pulled up her video footage from her drone. Then she pulled up seven pictures of marijuana in different stages of growth from an inch tall to its full height. She had a program from her German friend, Henrik, that had some of the best facial and object identification software in the world and he'd gifted her with a copy. She entered her drone video footage and told the software program to look for plants like the seven pictures she'd found of marijuana plants. Then she sat back and stared at the computer screen while it thought.

Within five minutes she heard a ding and she thought, *good that will be the field I found.* That verified for her that the software was on track and she sat back checking her email while the program finished. Then she heard a second ding and a third, and she thought darn the object identification software isn't good with plants as that was too many dings.

Sometime later the program finished and she focused on the screen to look at the object matching.

"Oh my gosh!" she exclaimed to the dog who was sound asleep at her side.

There were additional fields that she hadn't originally spotted in Lucy's video footage. This was a game changer. She zoomed in on the field the software identified as pot. Sure enough, the software was better than her own eyes at spotting the herb. She identified the Geo-coordinates of the fields and looked for their ownership, then she stopped to make a quick call to Angela.

"Hey Henrik's software is once again, brilliant! I ran the footage from my own drone through the program and it identified fields I hadn't viewed as marijuana initially. All I need now is footage of the Louisiana coast. Have you found a source?"

"You think I work that fast? We spoke just thirty minutes ago."

"Yeah, I do. You're fabulous with pictures. What have you found?"

"Ha! It just so happens you're right! I went to the National Hurricane Center and they have lots of footage of the Louisiana Coast as you suspected. I also found more from the National Oceanic and Atmosphere Center. Give me another hour, to find all the links for you and then you can run it through the program."

"You're the best!"

Jill glanced at her watch and returned to looking up property ownership. She'd calculated that the earliest bad guys could arrive from New Orleans was one in the afternoon, then they would have to get a rental car and make the drive to the Palisades Valley, which took another hour. So any efficient criminal would be arriving in her town about now. Then she had a bad thought – what if they went after Nathan? She picked up her phone and called.

No answer, he must be in a client meeting so she left a message, reviewing her travel calculations and asking him to make sure that he had his security system turned on.

Now, she returned to the new addresses she had containing marijuana. She dropped an email to Briggs and Heyer about her findings and asked for their assistance in searching for ownership. She was always curious about what the tax records would show for these properties. Those records were public and she could find them on her own, but the process she would have to go through to get that information would probably be delayed by a week or two depending on whether she could get it through the Internet or by snail mail.

Her phone rang and the caller ID said 'blocked'. Normally she didn't answer those kinds of calls, but given the timing, it might be the detectives.

"Hello."

"Jill, this is Detective Heyer. Got your email and we're looking into your property records. I'm surprised that the software you mentioned isn't used by the Drug Enforcement Agency. Seems like an easy way to find illegal pot fields."

"I suspect the problem might be the cost of software. My copy was gifted when I solved a murder for the CEO of the company that manufactures the software. I can give you that information if you think your agency might be interested in purchasing it."

"If the DEA can't afford it, then I'm sure the New Orleans Police Department can't afford it," Heyer said and Jill could hear the smile in her voice. "Before I forget, let me thank you for all the work you're doing for this case. We would find this information ourselves, but it would have taken a lot longer than it seems to take for you."

"I'm motivated to help you. I met with my local Sheriff to discuss the details of this case. I unfortunately dragged his department into protecting me in previous cases. In one of those early cases, his main Sheriff station was shot up by some bad dudes. I was inside the station at the time and they were just protecting me. So he'd really like me to close this case quickly."

"Despite all the weird cases I've been involved with in New Orleans, I'd love to share a beer with you if you ever return to my city. I bet you have far more fascinating stories than I do," Heyer said.

"You would be amazed. Meanwhile, I have my sophisticated security system turned on at the moment guarding my vineyard, my dog, and I. I left a message for Nathan as well to make sure his security system is on. By my calculations, any bad dudes that left New Orleans to track me down in California should be approaching my town at any minute. My town sees significant wine tourism, so strangers don't stand out despite it being a small town.

"Back to the case at hand, one of my team members is collecting satellite and aerial photographs of the Louisiana coast. Later today, I should have a complete listing for you of all farm fields growing marijuana on your coast. Another team member is putting together a dossier of sorts about the Senator and the companies that own these plots of land. It would help me if you would notify me as you locate each landowner based on the tax records.

"And now I'm going to step way over the line of my knowledge, respect, authority with your department and suggest that you and Detective Briggs bring the FBI into this case. I did a Google search on Louisiana and I'm amazed at the number of sheriffs, judges, and politicians in your fair state that have been indicted in office for criminal behavior. I worry that this Senator could quash this case through her connections in the state."

"Actually Jill, Detective Briggs and I were discussing that earlier today. Like you, we see that the Senator has many tentacles in the state and we're wondering where they reach in our department. Obviously to call in the FBI requires approval through the chain of command in our department and we're not confident that the chain of command is trustworthy."

Jill appreciated her honesty and the difficulty of their position so she offered a suggestion.

"Detective Heyer, over the past three years or so, the Special Agent in Charge of the San Francisco office has partnered with me on a few cases and connected me to other offices of the FBI. I think you may have spoken to her in reference to me when I first came on the case. How about if I contact her and request her help for my own personal safety. It takes you two out of the loop if I do that. When the FBI does come calling, your relationship with them may be somewhat inhospitable."

"I can't tell you to do that Jill, but..." Heyer said getting her point across but not saying anything.

"Well, I tried. Keep me posted on those property owner names."

They ended the call shortly after that and Jill put a call into her contact Leticia Ortiz, Special Agent in Charge. While Jill waited to get through the FBI switchboard to Agent Ortiz, she thought back to their relationship and the assistance that the agent had provided over the years with both helping and protecting Jill. Yes, she would call the agent a 'friend'.

"Hello Jill. What problem in your life are you having now?" said the agent when she came on the phone.

Jill laughed and replied, "It's nice that you believe my stories about criminals and criminal behavior, rather than seeking to get me locked up in a psych ward for my vivid, paranoid imagination."

"Hey I have no complaints, your cases usually bring me positive recognition from the higher-ups in my organization. What can the FBI do for you today?"

"I have a political corruption case in Louisiana."

"That's good, but that's not my geographic area of responsibility. Is there a reason you're not calling one of the seven offices in that state?"

"Yeah, it was a Google search that showed something like forty-eight elected officials including sheriffs have been indicted for public corruption. I don't like that and I have a trust issue there. Besides, I'm worried that the bad dudes may have followed me back to California. There were three attempts on my life while I was in New Orleans."

Jill could hear the rustling of paper and clicking of a keyboard in the background of the agent's office. That sound alerted her to Agent Ortiz becoming engaged in her case.

After taking a deep breath the agent said, "I can see now this is going to be a long and complicated story and before I refer it to my colleagues in Louisiana, I'll make sure I can trust them. Before you tell me your story, are you safe at home? I assume you're calling me from home given the area code that my phone says your call is coming from."

"Yes I'm safe at the moment, but I have my security system on and I know that the earliest time the trouble could follow me on a commercial flight from New Orleans is about now. Hopefully, my day is quiet," and with that Jill continued with an explanation of the case.

"Wow, death by evil spirits? I can see how that would capture your interest."

Jill continued with the story with the agent asking questions to clarify Jill's explanation. There was silence after she finished her story and Jill knew the agent was thinking about next steps.

"So you think these employees, hired by the Senator to silence you, know your name?"

"I do. They got a picture of me at some point and they followed me in Louisiana so I think they could've found out who I was based on facial recognition software, or talking to our car rental agency, or the airboat rental, but I don't know any of their names."

"So it won't do us any good to get passenger lists."

"No, and if they were smart, and they haven't been so far, they could take a flight out of New Orleans to any US destination, change airline companies, and hop aboard a different flight to my local airport, or land at San Francisco or Los Angeles. Impossible to trace all of those passengers."

"Maybe they won't follow you to California, but I'm guessing your security system will be the first alert. Have you notified your local sheriff?"

"Yes I met with him a few hours ago. Needless to say he's less than thrilled. He said he would personally fund my retirement party."

"Ouch!" laughed the agent. "I'm going to put aside your personal safety at the moment and let's talk about the political corruption. From what you explained, it sounds like you might have the fastest and potentially most accurate way to account for the illegal behaviors of this Senator."

"That's essentially what the two detectives have said in the NOLA PD. It kinda feels crazy, because on the one hand I live in a state with legalized marijuana so why am I offended by growing pot in Louisiana? But I'm irked for other reasons. The attempts on my life are a big deal. The fact that the senator is not paying property taxes because the land is owned by the state and it was declared 'underwater' and it's not. And then finally I looked at her voting record in regards to marijuana and she's done everything she could to keep it illegal which maximizes her profits on the crops she's growing on land she doesn't own. So that's why I'm bothered by someone growing pot."

"I hear you, Jill. I can confirm the FBI would agree with your desire to pursue political corruption charges in this case. Part of the issue here is the income from growing an illicit crop. If she sold 'organic' soybeans but used pesticides and she made $40,000 on that and owned the land; that's a far cry from a $3 million crop that is banned in her state grown on land she doesn't own. The first example is still corruption, but it's not growing illicit substances on stolen land. I've worked with some agents in the Louisiana offices, but I know that's a unique state as far as public corruption. I'll talk to a few people and find out who will be my point person there and we'll get rolling on the case. Meanwhile, if you have problems at your house and you have reason to believe that the bad dudes are from Louisiana or any other state, then my office will back up your Sheriff as it's now classified as an interstate crime."

"I was hoping you would take that action. That's exactly why I called. Keep me posted."

"And you likewise," said the agent as they ended the call.

Jill sat back pleased with all the little bonfires she ignited. This must be how an arsonist feels as they watched the flames grow. In her case, she was finding more and readily accessible data to take down the Senator. She couldn't wait to read emails from Marie or Angela on what they discovered. She also felt pleased that she had directed the FBI to the back door of this case. In fact she was very pleased with her day so far starting with the run that morning and moving on to the evidence collection. She was sure she deserved a glass of her wine at an unusually early hour for her. Oh well, as the saying went, 'It was four o'clock somewhere in the world.'

She was in her kitchen pouring the wine when she heard the first beep from her alarm system.

# CHAPTER 26

*S*ean Sharp had never been to California or seen a grapevine. They didn't have them in Louisiana. He supposed it was too wet to grow grapes in the south, or maybe it wasn't sunny enough. People talked really different here too. Since his plane landed, he had not found a single person with a southern accent. At least he found a country-western music station to listen to. And the traffic, he'd never seen anything like it. His boss had booked him on a plane that landed in Los Angeles. The airport had to be ten times bigger than New Orleans, he looked out the window while they taxied on the runway and saw planes going to far off places – China, Japan, Australia and New Zealand. When he was done with this job, he was going to go home and find those places on a map. He'd taken a shuttle bus to get a car rental, he wondered if he was on the wrong bus when it took ten minutes to reach the cars. Then his boss made arrangements for him to drive to a shady looking place just west of the airport where he could get a couple of guns and some ammo. It was all in the trunk of the rental car. He didn't know what this woman had done to make boss so mad, but it was the first time ever he'd been sent out of state to do a job.

At first, when he'd gotten on to a freeway, he wondered if there was a bad accident up ahead, the traffic was moving very slowly five or ten miles per hour. He looked around him and there were six lanes of traffic crawling slowly north. He liked the sun and the beautiful people, but this traffic was a nightmare. He wondered when he might finally drive out of it. There were no accidents, just a lot of people trying to go somewhere. Eventually after he passed an amusement park on the left, he sensed the traffic easing. His speed had picked up to the set limit of 65 mph. At first, he stayed at this speed because he didn't want any cops stopping him for speeding and finding the guns in the car. But when he had big rig tractor trailers passing him, he knew he had to speed it up. He tested his speed with the flow of car traffic and found he needed to do at least 73 miles per hour. He kept climbing uphill and he marveled at the mountains around him. There were no houses, yet there were eight lanes of traffic full of cars, weird. Then he saw a really scary sight, signs giving the distance to the runaway truck ramp while he'd been traveling downhill on a very steep grade. All of the big rig trucks were in the far right lane and had a posted speed limit of 35 mph. He'd seen a brake check area and wondered what that was for and now he understood. He was glad he was a professional hit man rather than a long-haul truck driver.

He'd reached the bottom of that massive mountain and the land looked flat for miles ahead and he could see he was driving through California's version of farming - huge cattle ranches, orange, avocado, and nut trees, sandy soil and tumbleweeds. It helped that the farmers had signs telling passing motorists what the orchard was growing. The lush greenness of Louisiana was nowhere in sight. His GPS indicated that he would arrive at his target location in about an hour and a half. Once he arrived, he planned to get the lay of the land and study his target's behavior. He hoped he could get the job done today as there was a 1 AM flight from Los Angeles home and he would need another four hours plus an hour and a half to dump the car and get through security at the airport. That timeline gave him four hours max to get the job done in this Palisades Valley.

He entered the town that seemed to be comprised of rolling hills and vineyards wherever he looked. There was a small Main Street with the requisite big grocery store in a strip mall off the main street. He passed a Sheriff's office that looked newly remodeled and followed the GPS to his victim's address. The land and buildings were so different from home, and the heat was so dry.

As he passed the open gate of the road leading to his victim's house he noticed the sign that said 'Quixotic Winery', and wondered if he had the right address. He sent an email to the boss to verify that the address of the winery was where his victim lived. While he awaited a response, he found a section of the road he could pull over on and use binoculars to further scope the layout of the land that might contain his victim at this very moment.

There were gently sloping rows of grapevines surrounding the house. The property also seemed to contain some barn type buildings and he wondered why she needed a barn as he hadn't seen any livestock in surveillance. He focused the binoculars on the windows of the house to see if he could see any movement. He wanted to assume that if the gate was open, she would be home. He had her picture on his cell phone and knew besides her facial portrait that she was on the short side about 5'3" tall with below the shoulders, blonde hair. He could see to the back of the house which looked to be bedrooms and a kitchen but didn't see her anywhere. He made another sweep of the vineyard and didn't see her out there. He would have to move onto the property to get a look at the front of the house. He debated taking his rifle with him, but decided he needed to perform surveillance without the weight of the rifle. Besides it was a good way to test the alarm system if there was one and not be caught with a weapon if he triggered some unknown security feature. He stepped on his intended victim's land, and he heard nothing, so he kept moving slowly. Just as he edged around the side of the house, he heard the sound of tires crunching on leaves and looked toward the gate to see a Sheriff's car turning in. Crap! he thought and turned around to run back through the vineyard to his car. He heard the sound of voices and a dog barking from behind him as he reached for his door handle. Seconds later he was belted in and moving down the road at a speed slightly greater than the posted limit.

When he was about ten miles away from Jill's house he pulled over and heaved a big sigh. He now knew she had some sophisticated security system that was invisible to the average intruder, or the arrival of the Sheriff's car was an extremely unlucky prescheduled event. He also knew he wouldn't be on the red-eye flight to New Orleans as he was going to have to scope this job out and confirm the presence of a security system. He gave some thought about how to detect the presence of a security system and decided to drive on to her property looking for a tasting room or a place to buy wine. Wasn't that what people did in wineries? If a cop showed up while he was there, he'd say he was looking for the tasting room. He would know that the land was wired, and had a silent alarm. Of course he could take a pistol with him and shoot her the moment she opened the door, but that might be caught on camera. Today's exercise would be to assess the cameras and confirm his target. Tomorrow, he would kill her and then as quick as possible head back to the airport and home.

He waited sixty minutes for the Sheriff to leave and then made the ten-mile drive back to her house. As he approached from the road he could see there was no longer a sheriff's car in her driveway. As he prepared to use his turn signal to turn into her driveway, he noticed the gate was closed and so he carried on past the house looking for another area to spy the house from. He spent another ten minutes driving roads to find a location which according to his map might give him an angle on her property, but he didn't find any. He hated these darn vineyards as they offered no protection to someone wanting to hide in them especially since it was fall and most leaves had dropped off the plants. He wished for some giant corn stalks for cover. He decided to go back to his original site and park along the side of the road. Before he got out, he scanned the area for cameras. He wanted to make sure he'd tripped a security wire at some time upon entering her property and not while he was standing there on the side of a city road. Seeing none, he pulled his baseball cap lower on his face and got out of the car again nearly two hours later from when he last scurried into his car to beat a retreat. Again he looked for cameras and saw none. From behind his glasses he scanned the properties looking for security devices and came up empty. He then moved his gaze to the house where he could see cameras covering several angles. He again pulled out his binoculars and studied the house, but he saw no activity at all and no car in front of the garage where there had once been one. She was gone.

# CHAPTER 27

When Jill heard her alarm ping, she called 911 and then went over to her screen to look for whatever activity set off the alarm. Once in a blue moon, she had tourists who would park in the road lay-by and either try to sample her grapes or would position themselves next to her grapevines for a photo shoot. She installed a sophisticated alarm system two years previous when she'd began to have her first trouble with bad dudes associated with her cases, then later she'd upgraded it further to have a camera on the lay-by. The cameras were painted the same color as her grapevines and were hard to detect.

She watched a man exit his car on the lay-by. He likely wasn't a tourist as they came in pairs at a minimum. He had a baseball cap on and stood looking downhill toward her house. It wasn't a steep downhill, rather a gently sloping row upon row of grapevines. She could see part of his face as her cameras were shooting up but his eyes were shaded by the cap. Hopefully as he got closer, a different camera angle would get his full face. She looked at his hands to see if he was carrying a gun, and his hands appeared empty. He was wearing a lightweight black jacket and she studied those pockets when he moved, but didn't see anything of weight moving. He could wear a shoulder holster under that jacket, but it would be for a small caliber gun.

He was getting close to the house, when she saw a sheriff's car turn in her drive. She let out the breath she hadn't realized she'd been holding. She had options to defend herself, but nothing like the firepower of that squad car. She watched the man peer around the corner of her house to see the car's approach, and he exited her property in a far greater hurry than he'd approached it. He reached his car as Jill opened her door to the deputy.

"Hello ma'am, I'm Deputy Mason. You called about an intruder on your property?"

"Hello Deputy, come on in and I'll show you the footage on my security system. The intruder must have noticed your car and hastened back to his car."

Jill pulled up the footage on her monitor for the deputy to view.

"We were briefed that you might have activity on your property and our patrols in this area were increased for the time being. Is this intruder, related to your case in Louisiana?"

"I don't know. Can you run his plates to determine who he is? I have on occasion, tourists that step onto my property but they come in pairs or more and they pause to take pictures with the grapevines. This guy didn't take any selfies."

Jill returned to the beginning and looked for a good view of the car's license plates and froze the frame with the best shot. The officer wrote it down and returned to his car to do a search on it.

He returned to her in no time and said, "It's owned by a rental agency near the Los Angeles airport. It will take us some time to identify who the renter is. Ma'am, I'm unable to stay with you for my shift; I need to be on patrol. Is there somewhere you could move in town to take you out of the immediate danger of this individual? Your security system can be viewed from anywhere, right? I will return if you stay and call for help, but I can't guarantee a response time that may be less than the time it takes for this man to move onto your property."

Jill thought about her options for a moment. She wasn't one to hide, but this man appeared to be an 'active security risk' and it would make sense for her own safety to move out of the way rather than being a sitting duck for him. She dropped Nathan a quick text to say she was moving in due to problems at her house. Overall, he'd likely be happy with that strategy as he saw her taking too many risks and he wanted to naturally protect her.

While the Sheriff waited, she packed a bag, grabbed Trixie's stuff, checked her land to make sure all cameras were working and her software system loaded onto her laptop and then the deputy waited for her as she closed and locked her driveway gate. They parted ways and Jill arrived at Nathan's about fifteen minutes later. When she pulled up to his house, she dropped her bag inside the door and left Trixie in his house with Arthur, Nathan's cat. She then walked the quarter mile on his land to his studio. Sure enough there was a car parked there that she didn't recognize. That meant he was still with his afternoon appointment, so she planned to walk over to chat with the employee that ran the printing side of his business, but was stopped when her phone vibrated. It was an alert from her security system that someone had briefly stepped on her property. She paused and looked up for shade in the area around her. The sun was too bright on her screen for her to see clearly. She walked over to a tree in the shade and was standing there watching the action at her house when Nathan walked his client out. He finished seeing the client to his car and then walked over to where Jill was standing.

He'd studied her as he walked and said, "Are you watching your security system at your house? Did you make the wise decision to move to my house for a while?"

Not looking up she said, "Yes and sort of."

Nathan leaned in and studying her phone's screen asked, "A lost tourist?"

Without looking up she said, "Nope, a man who approached my house via the vineyard after renting a car five hours ago from a car agency near Los Angeles Airport. A single tourist would never choose to stroll my vineyard as their likely first activity upon reaching this wine growing area. Also just as he reached the side of my house, Deputy Mason arrived and he changed his mind about that stroll and hightailed it to his car."

"So what is sort-of?"

Jill looked blankly at him for a moment and then smiled, "Deputy Mason convinced me to move here for the interim, it wasn't a thoughtful, wise decision on my part, more like complying with the deputy's wishes."

"He sounds like a good man."

"Yes he responded quickly and was informed and helpful. Now my worry is that I bring danger upon you and your business. Do you have all of your professional stuff backed-up offsite somewhere? I'm worried about this guy and the organization behind him."

"Not to worry, everything including my recent meeting with a client that ended ten minutes ago is backed up offsite. I think I told you once about the loss of a drawing early in my career and ever since, I've never lost a single piece of business data."

"What's your alarm system like here? I know what it was like two years ago, but I don't know if you made any upgrades. Are any of your cameras aimed at the boundary of your property so we can see who enters?"

"Yes, while I was meeting with the client, I got an alert on my cell phone that you had entered my property. Even the back area, where there is no wall, there are cameras on it. We're good here. If your bad dude manages to shoot up my printing equipment, that will set me back a month or so while I get replacements, but it's not the end of the world and it's covered by insurance. Is Trixie settling in with Arthur?"

"She's probably terrified up at your house. Now that that client is gone, I can probably let her out, as soon as you close the gate."

Nathan pulled out his cell phone, tapped the screen a few times and said, "Done. The gate is closed and the front door is presently open if Trixie and Arthur want to come outside."

The couple had started walking back toward his business as he wanted to say a few words to his printer. From there, they spotted Trixie heading their way as they walked towards Nathan's house. Her arrival was acknowledged by both of them, and she moved off the road to explore Nathan's property as they walked.

Once they entered his house, Jill showed him the video coverage from her security system.

"I wonder how long it will take for him to follow you here? I'm more worried about protecting you than myself or my property. I suppose someone could have snapped my picture while we were in New Orleans and since identified me. If they didn't, you're safe here for the foreseeable future. Let's put your car in my garage so it's not visible and I think you should avoid leaving my land until this man is caught. What would you like for dinner?"

Nathan was a great cook and that was always an advantage when she stayed at his place. She felt that he prepared anything she ate at a restaurant.

"Since I sprung myself on you, I'll leave the choice to you. Whatever you make, I'm sure it will be delicious."

As they approached his front door, Arthur was guarding it and swishing his tail to indicate his displeasure with Trixie's arrival. It was always that way with these two animals. They entered the house and headed into his kitchen where he had a massive kitchen island. Jill grabbed her laptop and settled in at the island. She loved watching Nathan work and just stayed out of his way.

He looked in his refrigerator deciding about dinner and then left and went to his wine cellar for a bottle of wine. He came back with a bottle of red which gave her insight into their dinner.

Her phone sounded the alarm again that she had a visitor. It was getting dark and she knew that the light went on automatically. She wondered if he'd come back looking for her to return. Once he started down the vineyard, she called 9-1-1 to get a Sheriff to come to her property. Dispatch stayed on the line with her giving feedback on the intruder's movements. There were two patrol cars a minute away and she requested one head to the lay-by where the man's car was parked. Jill sent a link to the dispatcher so she could relay the man's actions to the officers. Jill stayed on the line and winced as she saw the man break a window in her garage and enter it.

"Crap he just busted the side door window of my garage. He must think that will give him entry into the house."

Nathan asked, "Do you have cameras inside your garage?"

"I do and I can open the garage door from here, so as soon as the Sheriff parks and takes a position behind their patrol car, I'll lift the door. That is as long as he doesn't manage to break into the house. It's a solid door with deadbolts, hopefully it will keep him occupied for another ninety seconds which is the ETA of the patrol car."

Jill had a camera in the garage but since it was dark, she couldn't see anything until the suspect turned on the face of his cell phone; not the flashlight function, rather the light cast by the home page. Wise man as there was less light from that source. She and Nathan were watching the activity of different monitors around her property. They could see the Sheriff's car arrive at the lay-by, and then they saw the car pull into Jill's driveway. Using the coordination of the dispatcher and the deputy on-site, Jill opened her garage door once the deputy was armed and protected behind his patrol car.

They watched the suspect look surprised when the door began

to open. Then he assumed the shooter's stance ready to blast Jill as she parked her car in her garage. Except it wasn't Jill pulling in.

The deputy was ready, using a public address system to tell the suspect, "This is Deputy John Mason, come out with your hands up, do not make any sudden moves, and when you reach the end to the garage, kneel on the ground, and keep your hands in the air."

Jill and Nathan were holding their breath watching the deputy on one screen, and the suspect on another. Jill could almost see the wheels turning in the suspect's brain.

She said to Nathan, "He's going to bolt, I can just see it."

Seconds later she was right. The suspect approached the edge of her garage and made a sharp turn on the side he'd broken the window, and soon he was in the dark.

"I assume he's running back to his car," Jill said to the dispatcher with an edge of excitement in her voice.

She switched over to the camera covering the area where the suspect's car was parked as was a Sheriff's car. The deputy parked close enough to the suspect's car that he couldn't enter on the driver's side. The deputy had his gun out of the holster, using the car for protection.

"I've never seen all the bells and whistles on your system, it's really impressive," Nathan said.

"Then you'll be really impressed by this next option. When I installed the system, I knew there would not be much natural light in the vineyard at night and I also knew it's one of the greatest vulnerabilities of my property. So I have low light cameras staged there and we should be able to see if the suspect is returning to his car."

Jill switched to another screen of her security system and sure enough spotted the suspect moving through the grapevines. She gave that information again to the dispatcher.

Nathan was tracking the screen that had shown her garage and said, "Looks like the first deputy is leaving your house to go to the aid of the second deputy up on the road."

"Good idea," and then the dispatcher let Jill know that a third deputy was arriving on the scene, "That's two good ideas."

Jill had sent a second link to the dispatcher so that she now had the same view as Jill of her vineyard and could direct the deputies on scene as to the suspect's movements.

Fifteen minutes later, the three deputies had corralled the suspect and had him in handcuffs in the back of one of their patrol cars.

Jill's heart had been pounding since she had watched the suspect break the window into her garage. She wasn't in danger, but criminals always made her heart beat faster. She made arrangements through the dispatcher to meet the deputies at the Sheriff's station to see if she recognized the man and hear what he had to say. Of course he could refuse to tell them anything pending an attorney arriving on the scene.

# CHAPTER 28

Angela had been searching satellite images for the Louisiana coast and documenting the locations the images could be found on the Internet. It felt like redundant work to then have Jill go back and retrieve each image that Angela had just retrieved. So she came up with an idea to make it go faster. Jill gave her access to her computer, so that as Angela found the images she could run it through the software to look for marijuana plants. So far it was working splendidly, although Jill had texted her that there was police activity at her house and her security system screens would be consuming a lot of her RAM which might prevent Angela from using the identification software. Jill had indicated that the police activity would go on for an hour at the most. So Angela checked with Marie to see if she was available for dinner figuring the two of them could discuss the case and perhaps come up with some new angles for Jill.

After a hug, they sat down to dine. The restaurant was nearly halfway between the two of them. It always had excellent wine and a menu to cover any level of hunger. Best it had a couple of tables for two, that were in alcoves with swag drapes. There was not a romantic dinner for the two women rather it was a great way to have privacy while talking about murder.

Marie had chicken zucchini enchiladas while Angela chose spaghetti squash with meatballs. It was a great way to mix nutrition and taste. They started with a side salad of mixed greens with a vinaigrette dressing. Angela described her work documenting the marijuana fields of coastal Louisiana. She'd found eight pot fields and knowing their retail value, she marveled at looking at $24 million of farmland production. Marie spoke of the sophisticated spiderweb of corporations that Jill was tangling with. Angela described the story of the police activity occurring at Jill's house at the moment.

"Does she have any low-key cases anymore?" Marie asked. "It seems like every case in the past year has turned violent on her. I remember the good old days where she went in and did an autopsy found some weird diagnosis, gave it to the cops and that was that. There was no work for us and her cases were open and shut. Now she's tangling with foreign criminals, or hidden corporations, or psychos. Maybe that's the cost of fame."

"Maybe . . . Or the world has become a lot darker and more violent."

"I've finished researching the first couple names she gave me and to me just the mere set-up of the secrecy of these corporations makes me suspicious. I'm guessing that now you've identified another eight pot fields, that I'll have another new bunch of corporations to research. What do you think the turnaround time is for Jill to identify the property owners?"

"I think she has to coordinate that with the police from a timeliness perspective. If she went after the information herself she could get it, it's public information after all. However by the time they responded to any of Jill's requests it would be one or two months from now and she might well not be alive."

"True," Marie agreed. "However, my money's on Jill. She now

has a sophisticated security system and she has Nathan and she finally got her black belt in Tai Chi."

"Besides she survived all these other murderous crooks we've been running down."

Angela got a text then informing her that the police activity was over and she could again use Jill's laptop remotely to look for pot plants in Louisiana. She texted back for details on the police activity and Jill wrote back.

'Had guy try 2 break into house 3 times today. W/ help of my security system, deputies corralled him in vineyard & he's at the police station waiting 4 questioning. No hair on my head or Nathan's harmed during event. I've got fab security system & if either of you have trouble w/ bad people let me know & I'll duplicate system at ur homes.'

Angela read the text to Marie and they both chuckled.

"As if any trouble ever comes to Green Bay Wisconsin, except when our quarterback breaks his collarbone," Marie said.

"Gotta agree there. This is the first time in eight or nine years when our season has been over before the end of the regular season. Makes you want to hurt that defensive player that crushed his collarbone into the turf."

"Angela, I've never seen you even hurt a fly, let alone a 300 pound defensive player."

"True, and now I'll probably have to go to church confession for those evil thoughts, but it felt good for about ten seconds."

"Okay let's get back to the case, and maybe I'll have some coffee as I'm starting to feel like this will be a long night. You've discovered eight pot fields and Jill is going to have to call her contacts in Louisiana and they'll have to look up the ownership of the land. I bet the assessor's office isn't open at this hour, so they must have some special police source for knowing who's living at a certain address. Wonder if I could find anything on the Internet, I think I'll go home and research that."

Later, Marie found herself searching for ways to find the

assessors records online. A federal law gave law enforcement access to all assessor records, so the information had to be online somewhere she just needed to find it. She debated entering the dark web. In the Internet, the dark web was the lowest of low places. She could buy stolen credit card numbers, immortality substances based on fake science, illicit drugs of her choosing, a 3-D printer that could make guns or credit card skimmers, she could buy lottery numbers based in bitcoin currency, and she bet she could buy assessors database information if she looked hard enough. After spending forty-five minutes there and following various trails, she landed on a source. She studied a map of Louisiana parishes and there were ten by her count that touched the Gulf of Mexico.

She sat back trying to determine what to do next. Given the darkness of the dark web, she actually felt like she needed a shower after visiting the various sites. She could purchase bitcoins, and then use those bitcoins to purchase assessor information. She would end up with the whole state of Louisiana, and that might be useful if the senator owned land in other places of the state other than the coast. Jill's New Orleans detectives might wonder where she got the information, so she'd have to be sure that Jill had a story about a friend in the assessor's office. Not a likely story, but one that the detectives would probably ignore for the bigger picture of this case. She made her purchase of bitcoin and then went around the curtain and into the dark web.

Thirty minutes later she had all the information she needed. She downloaded the spreadsheet and exited the dark web. She went to her living room window to see if there was a FBI truck in front of her house, but fortunately, the street was empty. She washed her hands, and grabbed a cup of fruity tea, her compromise between coffee and wine. She informed Jill of her purchase and Angela of success, so now she just needed parcel numbers.

# CHAPTER 29

*J*ill was about to leave for the Sheriff's station to meet the man who had tried several times to break into her house. Just as she was getting into her car, she saw the email from Marie describing her success in the black web as well as an email from Angela stating she found eight coastal marijuana farms so far. Her friends had joined forces and were working through the evening and into the night on her behalf. Whether they were paid on a case or not, they always delivered the goods. Jill knew she was lucky to have such friends. By morning, she'd likely have the evidence for the detectives and their District Attorney, or maybe since the FBI was involved, they would use a Federal Prosecutor out of the Department of Justice. Regardless, Jill's team was collecting substantial evidence.

She arrived at the Sheriff's office where her burglar was in custody. She wondered if he'd been identified and if he answered questions or asked for an attorney. The police force was small in her town and likely the Sheriff himself as well as one of his officers would be doing the questioning.

At the front entrance she was directed back inside and was met in the corridor by one of the deputies she recognized from her home security system. After thanking him for saving her house from further damage, they moved on to the interview room, where she could stand at a one way mirror and both view the interview and listen through a speaker set up to the side of the window.

She asked the deputy, "Has he said much so far?"

"No, but I think he's thinking about a deal offered by our District Attorney."

"A deal?"

"Yeah, he was read the charges against him including unlawful possession of firearms and knows he could stand to do up to six years for the burglary and up to twenty for the weapons charge in a State prison in California. He's got a strong southern accent and so he knows he'll be doing time far away from his family. That's an incentive to cooperate."

"Have you identified him?"

"Yes his fingerprints were on file from a stint in the military, but he has no prior criminal history."

"What did he do in the military?"

"He was in the infantry and had the skill to be a sharpshooter but he chose to pursue a life in private," the deputy said while listening to the interview. "That sounds like he accepted the deal. Good."

Jill thought of the shots in the cemetery and guessed he'd been warning her to get out of town or leave the case alone. Sounds like he had the skill to hit her if he'd wanted.

"Can you ask the Sheriff to ask him a question?"

"Yes, I'll pass it to him on a piece of paper. What's your question?"

"Did he obtain the identity of the woman that was with me at the cemetery?"

The deputy wrote the question down and she could see him passing it to the Sheriff. He read and nodded and the deputy left. The Sheriff continued with the path of questioning he'd been using before he received the note; he'd add her question toward the end.

"Did he ask for an attorney?" Jill asked the deputy.

"We let him sit for about two hours while we discussed the case with the D.A., so we had some maneuverability with him. Up to this point he's declined an attorney. He's very interested in serving minimal time back home in Louisiana and we could arrange that for him with a plea bargain deal. Since he made his initial decision to talk, he has waived having an attorney present three additional times. He just wants the process over and to be escorted back home. Right now we're trying to determine who hired him. He's cooperating to the extent he can, but who knows if he knows anyone's real name."

"What's his name?"

"Sean Sharp."

Jill thought back to her trip to New Orleans and couldn't remember meeting any Seans. Then she thought of two other questions for the suspect. She'd assumed that Sean was the one that shot at her in the cemetery when she heard of his sharp-shooter skills, but maybe not. So she would ask that as well as if he was involved in the chase through the swamp. Answers to those questions would give her a sense of the scope of the Senator's operation. She dictated the two other questions and then quietly listened to the interview. The Sheriff was concentrating on who had hired Mr. Sharp.

"Who contacted you for this job?" asked Sheriff Arstand.

"Huh?" replied Sean Sharp.

"Who told you to go to California and find Jill Quint?"

"I got a phone call."

"On your cell?"

"Yes."

"Male or female voice."

Mr. Sharp gave him a puzzled look and replied, "Male." He'd never had a female ask him to do a job.

"When did you get the call?"

"Yesterday morning."

"Did you make your travel arrangements or were they made for you?

"They were made for me. I've never been out of Louisiana except to go to Gulfport. This state is too full of people. I'm never coming back."

"That's good to hear," said the Sheriff. "Were you involved in a shooting in a cemetery or in a swamp with Jill Quint in the last week? Since we offered you a plea deal and you accepted, then if you admit to these additional crimes against Dr. Quint, it will not affect your plea deal. We only want the truth."

"I hadn't heard of Jill Quint until the phone call yesterday and I wasn't in a cemetery or a swamp in the last couple of days or even in the last month."

Jill, listening, said to the deputy, "I wonder how big a group of criminals the senator employs?"

He didn't have the answer so they went back to listening to the interview. As they stood there, Jill heard another arrival to this part of the police station. She smiled when she saw it was Special Agent Leticia Ortiz from the San Francisco office of the FBI with two additional agents. The shook hands while Jill introduced the Special Agent to the deputy and she joined them at the window.

"I'd like to get into the interview room without breaking the Sheriff's interview rhythm. Is this a good time to tell him, I'd like to join him?"

"I don't know. I'll pass through a note to him like I did here with Dr. Quint's questions."

Ortiz looked at Jill and said, "You asked questions? I'm so shocked!"

"Haha. How come you're here? Isn't there a closer FBI office than San Francisco?"

"I had a call with our Stockton and Sacramento offices and while they're closer, they know I have prior experience with you and you're becoming something of a class 5 water rapid – getting involved in one of your cases is extremely difficult, violent, and can be the upper limits of what is possible to stay alive."

"Gee thanks. It's not my fault," Jill said with conviction in her voice.

"I know that and you've helped law enforcement all over the world take down some really bad people so we're grateful, but wary that this case is going to be the one that kills us or our agents."

Still Jill frowned at her response. Were her cases that dangerous? None of her or her team had ever spent a day in the hospital let alone been at risk of death. Sure Angela had been nicked by a bullet, and Marie and Nathan had been shot with a paralyzing agent, but they all fully recovered with only her, a doctor to the dead as their treating physician.

She tuned back into the interview room and saw that the Sheriff was taking a break with his interview and making arrangements for Mr. Sharp to use the bathroom, and get some food. Two deputies stepped in to escort the suspect out of the room, and the Sheriff motioned for Jill and the FBI Agents to follow him to a conference room.

After introductions were made, the Special Agent, who had met the Sheriff over one of Jill's prior cases began discussing strategy. Jill knew she had no role in the discussion or plan and she stayed in the meeting over worry about Jo's and her own safety. A representative from the DA's office also joined them.

Their conversation continued along the lines of further interview questions, transport and legal arrangements and then they heard that Mr. Sharp was ready for more interviewing.

Jill saw no role for herself in the conversation and said her goodbyes to the Sheriff and the agents. It was now late evening, dark outside, and Nathan had likely put dinner on hold waiting for word from her on when she would be home. She texted him and then turned the music off so she would have the silence to think on the short drive to his house. She was worried about Jo's safety and the answers from Mr. Sharp made it seem like there were many other bad guys out there yet no one else seemed to be worried about her safety. What should she do with her thoughts? Tell Jo? It was getting even later in Wisconsin and she'd hate to call her late at night. She'd talk it over with Nathan when she arrived; she needed someone to bounce ideas off of.

After greeting Trixie and Nathan and sitting down to a great glass of wine which she took a moment to appreciate, she discussed her issue with Jo's safety.

"Until the senator's organization is taken down, I'm afraid there might be an endless supply of criminals for hire to come after Jo and me. I'm really worried about her safety, but it's nearly 10 o'clock at night in Wisconsin and short of the police sitting on her doorstep I'm not sure what she could do at this hour."

"Is Jack staying with her? Does she have a second person in that house?"

Jack had been Jo's partner for the past five years or so and they were living together in Jo's house.

"Unless he's out of town for business or pleasure, then he should be at her house."

"Even though it's late at night it wouldn't hurt to give them a call and warn them. At the very least they need to lock their doors. She has a couple of dogs doesn't she, that will make noise if someone tries to get into the house?"

"She does, the dogs are small so no protection there, but they would give her some warning. Okay I'll give her a call."

She dialed Jo's cell phone and got no answer. That could mean she was asleep and didn't hear the phone ring or something was wrong and she couldn't get her phone. So she called Jack to see if he would pick up and fortunately he did.

"Hey Jack, it's Jill. Sorry to call you so late at night."

"What's up?" Knowing that Jill wasn't calling to chew the fat, he got right to the point.

"Is Jo in the house with you?"

"No, she stayed overnight in Milwaukee for a meeting."

"Okay... That's probably good, but you need to watch your back because you're in Jo's house I assume."

"That sounds ominous, who's after Jo?"

"I don't know that anybody is, but my house in California was attacked by a criminal from Louisiana today with an intent to kill me. He's in custody and admits no knowledge about Jo and I don't think he's lying."

"So why are you worried about Jo being in danger?"

"During the police interview of this guy, he seemed to have no knowledge of the shooting in the cemetery in which Jo was standing next to me. I'm worried that someone knows who she is and where she lives because her hotel room was searched. I think the senator that's behind all of this has endless resources to hire people to come after the two of us and frankly if she ever knows that Marie and Angela are working on the case, they'll be targets too."

"Maybe I'll suggest that she stay in Milwaukee another night. Do you think the senator might be in custody by then?"

"I don't know. It's up to the FBI to arrest her as one of their focuses is political corruption, but she's bought off a lot of people to grow these marijuana fields, or people are just unobservant in that part of the world."

"I think she has meetings in Green Bay later this week so I'm not sure how long she can stay in Milwaukee and still do her job."

"How about you Jack? As long as you're at her address of record, you're likely not safe. Can you move the dogs and yourself to a family member's house or a hotel for the next couple of days and nights?"

"I'll do a hotel tonight."

"By the way I tried calling Jo, but she didn't pick up her phone. I assume that's because she's asleep."

"Yeah, she can be a pretty sound sleeper, I'll talk to her in the morning about it. Anything else we need to know?"

"Be suspicious of anyone you run into with a southern accent. That's the only advice I can provide," Jill said with a smile in her voice.

They said their good nights and ended the call.

# CHAPTER 30

Senator Stephanie Harris was seated in her home office on the Black Oak Plantation, situated adjacent to the Mississippi River. The two hundred year old plantation reflected the grandeur of a time decades before the Civil War. It had been producing sugar cane for two centuries. She leaned back in a butter soft leather chair and stared out the windows at the fields. There were some thousand acres around the plantation planted in sugar cane, or at least the first fifty feet contained sugar cane crops. Once beyond the fourteenth row or so of cane, a different addictive substance, some would say, was growing.

Stephanie had taken over her parent's plantation at an early age after they were both killed in an auto accident. The plantation had been in dire financial straits at the time and she had to drop out of college and study the profitability of various crops, equipment and farm labor to figure out what to do. Then she was approached by a 'businessman' from south of the border with a business proposal. When she first heard of the proposal, she was outraged and said, "no thanks". The gentleman wisely did not take that to be her final answer and left his business card with her. He expected that he'd cycle back to her in six months and see if she would change her opinion as he expected, times would be tougher.

He was off on his calculation as she called in four months. She was ready to discuss a deal. His proposal was that Black Oak Plantation become an independent grower for Garcia Enterprises. She would retain full ownership of her property, but would grow crops to support his company. They were very interested in her land as it abutted the Mississippi River and her crops could be loaded aboard a barge and sent south to Mexico for processing before returning to the United States. She had been unaware of the second half of the equation at the time she agreed. She would also hire some Garcia workers to help her with the planting and harvesting of Garcia products. The product once harvested, would be put on boats to sail down the Mississippi River and out into the Gulf of Mexico and beyond for processing. Overall when she reviewed the proposal, she had no complaints, and her analysis anticipated the new crops would significantly increase her revenues. She liked everything in the proposal except the crop itself. It wouldn't wreck her land, but it would cause a problem if the crop was ever noticed. That meeting had been twenty years ago and so far no one had noticed the crops behind the corn and sugarcane. At least that had been the case, until Jill Quint had arrived on the scene.

Garcia Enterprises provided security for her crops which had expanded beyond the plantation to other pieces of land on the Gulf Coast of Louisiana. Their security resources extended beyond surveillance systems to informants and hackers in several state, local, and federal government agencies. She hadn't known about the murdered agriculture supervisor until she'd read the story in the Times-Picayune. When she first read the story, she' hoped it was some other grower's land, but then her contact from Garcia Enterprises had informed her of the problem. Now she had a feeling the whole scheme was about to blow up in her face and she would lose her land, her heritage, her status as a senator, and the respect of her state.

*Not if I can help it,* she thought and she reached for her cell phone.

"Hello," a single word with a Spanish inflection. No identification of who was on the other end of the phone.

"This is Stephanie," she said and then thought, how inane, he knew who was on the other end of the phone.

"Yes?"

"We have a problem."

"We will handle it."

"You've done a poor job of handling it so far. How many attempts have you made on this doctor and each is a failure?"

"You just worry about growing your crops for us, and we'll worry about everything else. That is our arrangement for the past twenty years, no?"

"I've done a superb job growing and expanding my production for you and now I'm left hanging in the wind, while you fail to uphold your end of the bargain. I have all the risk at the moment; my lands, my job, my reputation. You're not doing enough, nor are you quick enough to save this enterprise."

"Don't be hysterical Ms. Harris. Have we not kept your plantation safe for two decades? We have people in all the right places to make sure this inquiry goes no further."

"Know that if I go down, I'll take Garcia Enterprises with me."

"Is that a threat?"

"No, simply a consequence if you don't fix this problem in the next forty-eight hours or so."

Stephanie heard dead space from her phone and realized he'd hung up on her. Apparently, he didn't like her conversation. She'd been pacing the entire time during the call, and now she plopped down in her chair, closed her eyes and thought about what she could do to prevent the incoming tsunami. Who would get her information as to whether the authorities were close? Perhaps she should grab her passport and head for Andorra, a country with no extradition arrangement with the United States. She'd searched for a country to escape to a couple of years ago thinking the day might come when she would need to flee the United States. She even opened a bank account in the country. Andorra spoke a mixture of Spanish, Portuguese, French, and Catalan, and since she spoke Spanish and French, she thought she would fit in.

As she sat in her office chair she wondered if she should be packing now and heading to the border, or was she overreacting? Garcia Enterprises had killed the agricultural inspector and made numerous attempts on Jill Quint's life. There was no way to connect her to those egregious actions, that was all Garcia Enterprises. But if someone exposed her crops, she would face a media circus unlike anything she'd ever experienced before. She had been elected to the state government and had fought hard to keep marijuana illegal in Louisiana. When the public found out about her acres of pot, she'd probably go to jail for something.... at the very least she was farming an illegal crop and would probably get charged with political corruption for her stewardship of anti-marijuana laws.

What should she do? In the past, she had faith in Garcia Enterprises, but not this time. She researched the woman on her trail. She was smart and tenacious and observant. She'd made waves already with the New Orleans Police Department and the FBI. Stephanie had contacts in both agencies and those contacts were uneasy with what they were hearing about her. They were so uneasy that they had stopped taking her calls. Yes it was time to go. She had money planted in banks around the world, but Black Oak Plantation was Stephanie's love and her heritage and that's what saddened her the most. When she got to her final destination in Andorra, she would monitor the news back home in Louisiana. She hoped to return home if it all blew over and didn't result in her indictment. She'd kept a suitcase filled with family mementos to take with her if she had to flee. Now, she spent the remainder of the day putting information on to flash drives and then destroyed the electronics. Stephanie kept a small boat at her dock on the river. It was seaworthy, as long as the weather was okay, and so she could spend several days making her escape to Mexico from which she would begin the journey to Andorra. She had a passport with Mexican citizenship that Garcia Enterprises had obtained for her five years ago when she'd had a better relationship with her contact. She paused to check the weather forecast and it looked fairly benign for the next week. Hopefully there wouldn't be high winds or waves as she was a poor sea traveler. She debated briefly about telling her contact with Garcia Enterprises about her decision to run, but she saw no upside to that. After dark, she'd head out on her boat down the Mississippi and be in the Gulf of Mexico by the next morning. Once there Stephanie had a list of small marinas to stop at for sleep and gas before she arrived in Tampico. She'd give her boat keys to someone in the town and wish them happy sailing before getting a ride to the airport for a flight to Cancun and from Cancun to Barcelona, Spain and then buy a car for the three hour drive to Andorra. Hopefully the United States justice system would fail to find her. She'd earned millions of dollars over the twenty year relationship with Garcia Enterprises and wouldn't have to work once she arrived in her new home, she was just incredibly sad to walk away from twenty generations of the Harris family caring for the plantation. It was sort of a self-service witness protection scenario, where one life ends and another begins.

Stephanie paused later that night at her dock. All preparations had been made, her boat loaded with the few possessions she planned to take with her. She made arrangements to pay all staff wages owed them. She looked sadly at the plantation, knowing it might never look as grand again as she figured the government would seize her property and destroy the marijuana crops. She realized she'd been staring at the old grand house with tears running down her cheeks, missing it even as she stood there looking at it, knowing that she could just stay and weather the storm. But she was a coward and cowards ran rather than face the consequences of their bad behavior. With a swipe of her eyes and blowing her nose, Stephanie turned her back and climbed aboard the boat to freedom. She hoped her personal pity party would keep her alert until the sun rose the next day just about the time she reached the gulf and her first stopping point where she'd get gas, and a few hours of sleep. Stephanie soaked in the sights and sounds of Louisiana for the last time; humidity, bugs, odors of sewage, oil, or chemicals on the river. She passed the bright lights of New Orleans and entered an area of darkness, lit only by other vessels on the river which was busy with commercial traffic. She passed large cruise ships and barges, but very few boats of her relatively small size. She turned her back on the city and sought to call up images of her new home in Andorra feeling alone on the river and in her life.

# CHAPTER 31

Ricardo Rodriguez had worked for Garcia Enterprises for nearly twenty-five years dealing with many contacts in the United States. He always had a sense of when a relationship was going south and he was feeling it now with Stephanie Harris. Their last phone call was the first time she'd ever been anything but the epitome of southern hospitality and that was a sure sign that things were going south in his experience. So he'd come back to her house late at night with the intent of doing it damage. It was his way of scaring his contacts into compliance. She loved that house and causing it damage was the best way to get her attention. He was responsible for all drug shipments to and from the lower Mississippi River and he had a large fentanyl and meth shipment boat that would be using her dock in two days. He needed her back under control and working for him. He started out wanting her land to grow pot. Now the margin on Chinese fentanyl was much better than that on marijuana and increasingly as more states legalized it, pot wasn't profitable. With California soon legally growing its own, his colleague that covered the western U.S. was seeing his profits dramatically drop. He needed the good senator for her dock. He moved eighty percent of his product through her dock and he thought it unlikely that she understood that. When they spoke it was almost always about the cultivation of her pot crops, not questions about why he made so many deliveries to her dock. He'd told her he was delivering bags of fertilizer to his men that made her pot crops grow faster and have higher content of the active ingredient in them. Actually, they were large plastic bags of illicit drugs that his men moved off her property and on to delivery trucks.

He stared up at the plantation from the river and wondered if she was there that night. He knew the layout and planned to start a fire in an area he knew to be at the other end of the house from where the bedrooms were and as he planned to call the fire department as soon as he saw that the house had caught fire, she was sure to not burn up in it.

Ten minutes later he paused with satisfaction looking back at the flames running up a corner of the building. He pulled out a burner phone and made the call to 9-1-1 reporting the fire without giving his name. As soon as he heard sirens he tossed the phone into the river and departed on his own boat. As he did, he noted that her private boat wasn't in its usual slot which was unusual for this time of night. Maybe she had it in a dry dock for some work. That was pretty routine for boat owners.

As he drifted out into the Mississippi, he headed upstream on the river side opposite the Black Oak Plantation where he had a good view of the emergency activity. He thought they had the fire out in under five minutes according to his view through a pair of binoculars. *Good*, he thought, just what he wanted. Damage to her precious plantation, but not significant. He had room to make it much worse if she didn't cooperate quickly. Tomorrow, he'd send her a message in case she hadn't figured out that the fire was his work.

He thought back to her plea that he do something about Dr. Jill Quint. He hadn't heard from his man that he'd sent to California in thirty-six hours. Either he suffered an accident and died or he was in the custody of police. He needed to find out which scenario it was. If he was in police custody, he would let sleeping dogs lie rather than compounding it by sending someone else to do the job. Jill Quint had no knowledge of Garcia Enterprises he was sure; Stephanie's concern was she would be found out for growing marijuana. He called his colleague in the west to have him get the information on what happened. His colleagues would have contacts that could find out a lot quicker than him.

# CHAPTER 32

Jill woke up the next morning at Nathan's after an uneventful night. No alarms had gone off at his house or hers, nor had she got a call from Jack saying there were problems in Green Bay. Maybe the people after her had only one hitman or it was taking time to fly another person out to California in which case she could expect trouble by lunchtime. She would check in with the sheriff to see what else they had learned during the interview and maybe she could influence the FBI to provide Jo with some protection.

Sitting at the kitchen with a cup of coffee, Jill opened her laptop looking for messages from Marie and Angela. It had sounded yesterday like they had found a process to collect evidence and just needed computer time to gather the information for Jill. Looking at her inbox she saw their messages. *Bingo,* she thought after reading their emails this should be enough information for the authorities to detain and question the senator.

Jill reached for her cell phone to call agent Ortiz. She hoped she was still in the area.

"Yes Jill?"

Jill liked that the agent got to the point quickly not wasting her breath on social niceties.

"Two of my team members did some wonderful work overnight that I'd like to share with you. Are you still in the area?"

"I was on my way back to San Francisco, but I'm only about half an hour into the journey. I'll turn around and head to your house. Give me your address again so I can put it in my GPS."

Jill did so and looked forward to the agent's arrival in thirty minutes or so. That gave her time to write Nathan a note, gather up her belongings and Trixie, and head home before the agent got there.

She left her front gate open and entered the house to look at the security system making sure all of its components were live and working. She'd just finished the check, when she noted the agent's nondescript sedan enter her gate. She went over to her front porch, to welcome her inside.

"So what do you have?" Special Agent Ortiz asked.

"I have a list of fifteen Gulf Coast Louisiana plots of land that are growing marijuana. Many of those plots are designated as owned by the state because they're underwater which clearly they are not if they're growing marijuana. I also have a list of the corporations that own those plots of land. I'll leave your legal and accounting experts to follow the trail."

Jill opened the spreadsheets attached to the emails that Marie and Angela had sent for the agent.

"You remember Angela, the photographer, right?" Jill said beginning her explanation.

"I do," replied Special Agent Ortiz.

"I asked Angela if she could find through her photographic resources, pictures of the crops in Louisiana that are adjacent to the coast. I picked the coast because I thought that was where land that was deemed 'underwater' by the state was most likely located. There may be many additional crops grown inland."

"Got it."

"Once she found a source of images, then we use my software to match up the images to one of seven pictures relating to the age of the marijuana plant. Some plants are two inches tall and others are several feet and I needed to account for the different sizes and changes in the leaves as the plant grew."

The Special Agent nodded her head understanding the explanation.

"Once Angela identified the crops that appeared to be marijuana, she located the geocoordinates so they could be used to identify the owner. My other teammate, Marie, went to a location of the Internet that has her feeling slimy this morning. She was able to gain ownership records of those plots of land. So that's this spreadsheet," Jill said pointing to the screen.

Special agent Ortiz looked at the screen and nodded.

"These three properties at the bottom of her list are of special note. In doing research for this case, I read a lot of stuff about the erosion of the coast in Louisiana. With global warming, and the deterioration of the marshes, Louisiana as a state, is shrinking by sixteen square miles a year. Whole cities are being evacuated. One of the stories I read was about a Native American tribe called the Biloxi-Chitimacha-Choctaw that live in a city called Isle de Jean Charles. They've lived there since the early 1800s, but have lost so much land due to hurricane damage and rising sea waters, that the government is assisting them with moving elsewhere in Louisiana.

"When a plot of land slips underwater, the ownership of that land goes to the state and the original landowner no longer pays taxes or has the deed. That's not to say that the state is monitoring those lands individually. So the three properties on this list either were declared underwater incorrectly, or someone did something to reclaim the land and use it to grow pot. I read that you can reclaim land by taking sediment from the Mississippi River and dumping on land that you wish to reclaim."

"Wow, I suppose that could be San Francisco someday if our

oceans keep rising. So besides growing pot, the other problem is that they're stealing the land from the state in order to do so."

"Yes, and this final attachment is what really irks me. This is Senator Harris's voting record in regards to pot - recreational, medical, sentencing in the justice system - she's done everything she could to prevent pot from entering Louisiana through legitimate sources like medical dispensaries, and they have one of the stiffest penalties if you're caught with an ounce of pot on you. So I have a problem with the hypocrisy of her actions farming the land versus her actions as a senator. My friend Jo, the financial whiz, looked at her from a financial performance perspective. Her comment was that the senator's actions serve to raise the cost of pot for illicit users and served to maximize her profits for growing weed."

The Special Agent leaned back in the chair and contemplated everything that she just looked at on the computer.

Jill added, "What I don't know and can't know is who she has paid off to look the other way on her pot fields. I can't believe I'm the first one to discover them. Certainly local law enforcement should've seen them. Of course one of the things she does to hide these crops, she grows a different plant around the outside of a pot acre like corn or sugarcane. She'll plant several rows of corn that serve to hide the marijuana."

"Jill, would you email me your data? I'm going to need to talk it over with the Special Agent for New Orleans."

"Not to be rude, but be careful as you don't know who is on the side of justice and who is on the side of the senator. That state has a long history of politicians being charged and convicted of criminal behavior."

Special Agent Ortiz nodded and left Jill's house when she was assured that the data was in her inbox. On her way back to San Francisco, she'd call a few people in the offices of the FBI. Jill watched the special agent's car pass through her gate. She went back to her living room and asked herself the question - 'what now'? She readily admitted she knew nothing about the justice system, but she thought that the data that Angela and Marie had gathered was enough evidence to have something to charge the senator for.

She went back to look at her inbox to see if anything was there from the Sheriff. He said he would inform her of the highlights of the interview. She didn't know if whoever had hired Sean Sharp was done chasing Jill, or if it was a case of the next man up.

Searching the inbox, she saw the message from the Sheriff and opened it. Skimming the contents, Jill found no answers to the question of whether another hired gun would be after her. There was nothing more she could do about it, so she tried to focus on something else. After what felt like a month of ignoring her wine business, she decided to check on how the sales were doing with her latest vintage. It was her third year of bottling grapes from her land and the first two years had sold out in the local wine stores within two months of their arrival. She'd increased her production each year and so expected this year to be slower. Maybe it would take six months for her product to sell out, or maybe it wouldn't sell out at all if this vintage wasn't as good as the previous two.

An hour later, she felt like she was up to date on the winery side of the business. She sent each of her teammates a case of the recent vintage. It was her way of saying thanks especially as they occasionally did work for her for which they were not compensated. She noticed another email in her box from a colleague in the Kern County coroner's office. Someone had died in their county, but there wasn't a reason to perform an autopsy other than the family wanted it, so the coroner had referred the family to Jill. It was an FYI email in case she received a call. After the complicated case of New Orleans, she would almost welcome a routine autopsy from someone who died under no suspicious circumstances. Either she would get the call today for the autopsy, or tomorrow they would transfer the deceased to a local mortuary to free up space.

Jill then had a thought for Detectives Briggs and Heyer. While the case seemed to be under the wing of the FBI, she thought she owed the two detectives the latest information on the case. The land involved was not under their jurisdiction. The man that had tried to kill Jill on her own land wasn't in their jurisdiction either; he was returning to NOLA to serve his sentence. Still she didn't like leaving people out of the loop and so sent them an email of the recent happenings on her property and the data her team had collected. Briggs surprised her with a request to call at her convenience. Jill picked up the phone and dialed the number.

"Hello, this is Jill Quint."

"I figured it might be you, as no one else would be calling me from California. I was about to call you," Briggs said

"What's up? Something new on your end?"

"Just an unusual occurrence. The Black Oak plantation belonging to Senator Harris had a fire last night."

"Oh my! Did she perish in the fire?"

"The fire department is still going through that section of the house, but they found no human remains so far."

"Was it hot enough to cause her cremation?"

"No, it wasn't extensively damaged and it's on the river so there was plenty of water to put out the fire. No one has been able to make contact with the senator today. Her home is not in our parish so we're not assisting with locating her, but we're being kept abreast of developments."

Jill relayed the information on Sean Sharp and the thought that the FBI was closing in on the senator.

"I don't understand the justice system, but I believe that the FBI was about to request the senator's presence for questioning this week. It feels like she has spies everywhere, so perhaps she decided it was time to leave the United States."

"Maybe. The officers investigating the fire have said there

were no witnesses and her plantation is lightly staffed so no one would have seen activity around the house. She did have an alarm system and the local police are getting a warrant to look at the data in that system, so we'll know more later today."

"Interesting. Her main home was a plantation in North New Orleans?"

"Yes."

"Is there a dock connecting the plantation to the river?"

"I think so. Most of those old plantations have such a connection."

"Does she have a boat registered to her?"

"I don't know, but I get where you're going. You're suggesting we use the Coast Guard's boat tracking system."

"If we knew that she left by boat, then she might be traceable on the river. Of course, once she reaches the Gulf of Mexico, all bets are off unless she hugs the coastline and her radio signal is picked up by the same system."

"We'll look into those angles. Talk to you later."

Jill hoped the two officers would have success trying to use the Coast Guard system to see if she was on the river. There were so many variables on that angle, that the chances of it working were probably slim.

Jill relaxed her back and her brain thinking as far as she was concerned she was done with the case; there was no new information for her to locate, and at least at the moment, no one was trying to harm her. The case was a thousand miles away and it was up to the justice department to close the case. She took a deep breath and relaxed.

Stephanie Harris had been in Andorra for a week. She was settled into her new apartment if not to her life. At any given moment she was mourning the loss of her beloved plantation, her U.S. Citizenship, and the title, 'The Honorable Ms. Harris'. Given her criminal activity, she would never be allowed to run in an election and thus be called 'The Honorable' again. It had taken her a little over a week to reach Spain after she fled the U.S. She'd been constantly looking over her shoulder the entire time, thinking she wouldn't get away, but she did. Either she had enough of a head start, or they'd been unable to track her beyond Texas as she turned south and headed toward Tampico.

She hadn't looked any stories up on the internet for a variety of reasons; first and foremost she wanted to get away without detection and that meant using no cell phone other than one she purchased at each harbor and threw away at the next, but more important no check of her email or the internet.

Now that she was in Andorra, there was no way to trace her beyond Barcelona. As she paid cash for the car that she drove to her new country, she pulled on a wig and a decorative scarf that she'd packed in her luggage. She also had a set of fake license plates that she initially put on the car until she was fifty miles outside of Barcelona. At that point she removed them and the original plates were revealed, so she felt secure in her escape. By now as a public figure, her absence would have been noted and if the police weren't looking for her out of worry, they were looking for her as a suspected felon. But, she'd been in her new home a week and all was quiet.

Now she dared to look at the U.S. news. She chose the New Orleans Times-Picayune as she would be one of thousands of readers viewing their contents from an internet cafe in a foreign country. She entered her name into their search function and waited for news to be searched for her. She skimmed the news.

*'Damn that man!',* she thought.

One news story described a small fire that had broken out in the library wing. It had been extinguished quickly by the fire department who had received an anonymous tip about the fire. Her plantation had never in its two-century history had a fire. She'd bet it was her contact from Garcia Enterprises. Sure she had enemies in politics, but those enemies had had years to strike and she didn't believe in the coincidence of it happening on the day and time it did. It was the first time she'd snapped at her Garcia Enterprises contact. The article also mentioned that the police were looking for Senator Harris to follow up on the fire, and had been unable to reach her. So they knew she was missing, but apparently not where she had gone. There was no mention of her anywhere growing marijuana, but maybe the police hadn't found a reason to release that information. She leaned back in her chair and debated what to do next.

It was one thing for her to flee her grand plantation, but she'd left it in good shape so that when the state took it over it could be used for a park or they could sell it and probably recompense all the taxes she'd never paid for her marijuana sales. Now someone had damaged that pristine property and she wanted to strike back. Stephanie wanted to look something up that was on a flash drive when she left the United States. When she passed through Mexico on her way to her present location, she purchased a tablet computer. Now she'd go home and review her summary of services with Garcia Enterprises.

An hour later, she was reading a scanned copy of the document she'd been provided two decades ago. She'd done a search for information about Garcia Enterprises in Mexico. At first it had been very difficult as Garcia is one of the most common names.

She also wondered if any of the information in the document was accurate. They had not signed a contract as that would've been foolish as it was an illegal operation, but she'd asked when originally approached for a written document describing what Garcia Enterprises would do for her and the details of her payment schedule.

Over the years, activity on her land had changed, and she'd never been provided with the new document, nor had she asked. She'd been happy with the payments and had looked for more land to grow pot on. In the last five years, she'd come up with the scheme of reclaiming land that was underwater by packing it down with river sediment to make it arable land again. She found the plots of land, and her Garcia Enterprises contact had arranged the reclamation process. She got a percentage of the profits off of those lands - sort of a finder's fee.

Now as she examined the document supplied by her contact, she noted no names by which she could identify him or the enterprise. She tapped her fingers on the table as she sat looking at the tablet and then she had another idea. She remembered that she'd installed a security system almost a decade ago. When it was first installed, she'd captured video of him arriving at her dock. He noted the placement of the camera and had dismantled it before he left her house that day telling her never to place a camera on her dock again. She complied with this request, but kept the original video. Now she searched her files for that video clip and found it a half an hour later. She decided then and there she was going to try to take him down from four-thousand miles away. She located Dr. Jill Quint's website and email address. Stephanie bet that tenacious woman would take down the nasty man who had dared to harm her beloved plantation. It might not be hers anymore, but no one else was allowed to damage it. She began typing her email.

*Dear Dr. Quint,*

*This is Stephanie Harris. I fled the United States about two weeks ago when I sensed you were getting close. I chose a business partnership over twenty years ago to save my beloved family plantation. My parents died together in a car accident and I lacked the financial means to keep the property going. At the time I was approached by a man who said he represented Garcia Enterprises, a company from Mexico. Four months later, I found myself growing marijuana for export south down the Mississippi River to Mexico.*

*The income from that crop, allowed me to pay for the upkeep of the plantation and more. I eventually served our government trying to do the best for the citizens of Louisiana. I plan to live my life quietly in another part of the world, but I couldn't resist checking the news from home. I discovered that there was fire damage to my plantation, and I am angered by that. Never in two-hundred years was there a fire. I'm sure my contact from Garcia Enterprises was behind the fire and now I want to bring down his drug empire for the damage he did to the plantation.*

*I don't know his name, and even if he'd told me his name I wouldn't have believed him. I've attached a video from about ten years ago that clearly captures his face. Perhaps you can identify him.*

*Not only did he move marijuana south, but he may have been moving other product through my plantation to the rest of the United States. I say 'may' because he frequently had boats unload large plastic bags on pallets. When I questioned what was in the bags, I was told it was fertilizer for the marijuana plants; specifically to increase the content of THC. Over the years, I believe too many of these bags were delivered just to fertilize my land if you get my drift, but I did nothing further to confirm my suspicions.*

*Since you seem to have resources at your fingertips and contacts at all levels of law enforcement I forward you this video with the advice, that if you stake out my property - the Black Oak plantation, over the next two weeks, you'll be able to intervene and perhaps break up a large drug ring. It's the one parting gift I can give my country.*

*I would like to hear the outcome of this email. I'll be watching the online classified ads for the next three months in the Times-Picayune. Please leave word for me there, so that I may rest with the knowledge that my plantation is no longer in danger.*

Stephanie read the email a few more times. When she perfected it to say what she wanted to say, she made a copy on a flash drive and went out to her car. Three hours later she was seated in another Internet café in Toulouse, France in full disguise. She was dressed as someone's eighty-year-old grand-mother. She created a new email account, then sent the email to Jill Quint. Within five minutes, her stooped back was seen leaving the Café.

It would be the last time she was captured on video, for on the way home, she was killed by a wrong-way driver on the Auto-route 66. Her car was involved with a high speed head-on colli-sion that left both drivers dead.

# CHAPTER 34

Jill was back into the routine of running a winery. She'd done all the work of preparing her vineyard for winter and was evaluating whether to add a second grape to her vineyard. She was focused on a grape called Nero d'Avola. It was a red wine grape from southern Sicily that grew in a climate similar to the central valley of California where Jill lived. She liked red wine and thought she could be technically good at creating vintages with the grape. Her only concern was it was a strange pairing of sweet white Moscato and a fruity red. She really needed to add a few varietals to her winery and given that the plantings took five years to come into production, she really needed to be sure about her production. She could buy grape juice for any varietal and experiment with blending to see what she could achieve. She had two months before she needed to plant the grapevines, so she set about buying grape juice to experiment with what she could achieve. In addition to the Nero d'Avola grape, she purchased Barbera, Viognier, and Trousseau. She always liked Port and wanted to experiment with making the wine. Each of the grapes that she was purchasing liked a hot, dry climate to grow in and thus were suitable to her land and give her a mixture of red and white wines.

She spent time studying the various grapes as well as purchasing some ready-made wines to see if she thought she could improve upon them. She would discuss her choices with Nathan as it was his skill set to advise her on the branding and marketing of the various wines. Did she have a collection of wines that made sense as a group and would attract consumers? She sighed and finished with her business planning for the vineyard for the coming year.

She'd ignored her email for a while to concentrate on her business plan, but now it was time to see if there were any messages relevant to Jill Quint, forensic pathologist and private investigator. She scanned her inbox which was often filled with spam these days. People that needed her services as a pathologist always telephoned, so she wasn't worried about missing a client by ignoring her email. As she scanned down the list, she initially missed the email, but as she was going down and checking the left side box to delete a message without reading it, she saw it and opened it.

It was a startling email from Stephanie Harris. She read the words several times to assure herself of its contents and to think about her next steps. Ms. Harris was correct that Jill had contacts in law enforcement and that she would do something with the information in the email. First though, she was amazed at the woman's hypocrisy. On one hand she wanted to serve her country by breaking up a drug ring and yet she'd supported said drug ring for two decades. Jill was outraged by the woman's behavior.

After a pause to reflect on the strange morals of some of her fellow humans, Jill opened the attached video clip and played it. The woman was correct in that this was a good picture of the man. She opened her identity software to see if she could identify the man in the picture. The software came back with a name, in fact, seven names for the man's face. He was identified as Ricardo Rodriguez with an additional six aliases. He was on Interpol's most wanted list as well as the DEA. Her opinion of the dishonorable senator sank lower. This slime ball was her business partner for two decades? Unbelievable that she didn't know what was going on; the senator managed to wear a big set of blinders.

So who should she tell this news to – the FBI or the NOPD? Since the plantation was outside of the city of New Orleans, it would fail to come under the jurisdiction of the New Orleans police or its parish sheriff. Really, it was a DEA thing but she had no contacts there and she'd waste time legitimizing herself as a source. Beyond the email, and she had no way to verify that it was really from the senator, she supposed if she sent it to a computer expert, they might tell her an IP address which would correlate to a city that the email came from, but it wouldn't verify who actually wrote the email.

She decided she would spend a few hours building a dossier of sorts on this Mr. Rodriguez. If he had been coming and going from the plantation's property for two decades, Jill bet there was evidence of his movement in New Orleans. Especially since he visited her dock at times separate from his deliveries of 'fertilizer'. She doubted he could be flying in and out of the New Orleans Airport to transact business since he was on so many 'most wanted' lists. The river made a perfect way to enter and exit the United States, but it took time to sail from the Gulf of Mexico to the senator's plantation. It took even longer to move from Mexico to the head of the Mississippi. So either this wasn't his mode of transportation or he had a lot of time on his hands.

She returned to study airport security reading a few articles on it and it appeared that passport control connected to criminal databases and so that should have stopped his entry. However, the government was aware of aliases presumably because he used them. So what was to stop him from just using another alias to cross the border? She knew the TSA didn't use Henrik's software yet, so could she use a public cam at the airport to see if Mr. Rodriguez was passing through?

There were a series of public traffic cams on roads throughout the state and she looked at several of them, but the resolution wasn't good enough to identify drivers. There were other public cameras around New Orleans, but if you didn't live or work in the French Quarter, was it likely that you visited there several times a week? It would be like looking for a needle in a haystack. She was going to contact someone with access to the security cameras at the airport. That seemed to be her only option of reducing the haystack to a single bale. She picked up her phone and hit eleven buttons.

"Hello Dr. Quint," Briggs said when he answered his cell phone.

"Hey detective. I've got a weird request."

"Oh and all the other questions you had for us were routine?"

"Well, yes they were."

"Before you give me your request, the senator's case is closed."

"I don't understand, how did it close so fast? Did she confess and agree to go to jail?"

"No, she's dead. We received notice out of France that she was involved in a car accident and was killed. The officials tried to make a notification to the Mexican Embassy as she was carrying a passport that said she was a citizen of Mexico. They had no record of her in their system, and so using her fingerprints they determined who she was and called our embassy and notifications went from there. So we'll plow those Marijuana fields and that will be the end of that case."

"Do you know when she was declared dead?"

"Why, do you want to do her autopsy?"

"Ah, no. I received an email from her and I want to know if the send time is before or after she was killed."

"What!"

"Yeah, I got an email from someone who signed it 'Stephanie Harris'. I have no way to know who really sent the email, but a good starting place would be her time of death."

"Just a moment," Briggs said and Jill could tell he put his hand over the phone and said something to someone.

"Heyer will find the time of death. Tell me about this email."

Jill did as requested including her identification of the man.

"Wow, that's major and interesting news....So there's a major movement of drugs every couple of weeks through the dock on her property according to the late senator."

"Yes."

There were noises in the background, then Briggs came back on the phone. "The senator's time of death is listed as 14:46 CET. I guess that's the time zone in France."

Jill was googling the time zone and looking at the date listed on the email.

"It looks like she sent this email, about an hour before her death. I guess I won't be taking an ad in the Times-Picayune to tell her the man has been arrested."

"No I don't think anyone cares about the Black Oak Plantation at this point," Heyer said. Briggs must have put the call on speakerphone.

"So what are you going to do with this email?"

"Good question," Jill heard Briggs mutter.

"I have a good friend in narcotics. Let me talk to her. Can I call you back on your cell, Jill?" Heyer said.

"Yes, please do."

"Would you forward me the email?"

"I just hit the forward button. Do you see it in your inbox?"

There was a pause and she heard Briggs say, "Got it," and they ended the call.

She debated calling Special Agent Ortiz, but she didn't want to complicate things for Briggs and Heyer if they could do something within their own department to stop this flow of narcotics. She felt an urgency to do something though because she thought Mr. Rodriguez would move his criminal enterprise as soon as he heard of the senator's death. In her view, they needed a sting operation today. She'd give the two detectives an hour to call her back, then she'd go after bigger guns than the New Orleans Police Department. In her heart, she felt like they would drag their feet because they knew the plantation was out of their jurisdiction, but she'd called them because of the airport security cameras. She was lacking the patience to wait out Heyer and Briggs, so she ran upstairs to change into her running clothes and was out beating a path with Trixie at her side. She supposed she should worry about a hit man, but she rationalized her way to the belief that no one was after her.

Thirty-five minutes later she was nearing her house, her run nearly at an end, when her cell phone vibrated on her waist. Stopping, she pulled the cell phone out of the waist belt to see who was calling. It was a blocked number which probably meant it was Briggs or Heyer.

Gulping for air, she answered "Hello".

"Jill it's Heyer. I'm afraid it's a 'no-go' from our end. My friend in narcotics said that indeed if this is urgent to call the feds. Her unit is unaware of this transport route and they would have to verify its existence and then coordinate with their local narcs since this is out of our area. Personally, I think she's so overwhelmed by the workload inside the city, that pursuing something beyond the city is not going to happen. She gave me the name of the DEA agent in charge of this area for contact and I have a call there. If there's an arrest there, we'll let you know."

Jill had recovered her breathing by the end of Detective Heyer's explanation, but really had nothing to say. She was disappointed, but understood the narcotics detective's rationale. They ended their call and Jill debated what to do next. There was only one person she could call. She approached the front steps to her house and went inside to grab a towel to wipe the sweat from her face. Then she sat down on her porch steps, Trixie at her side with a look of dog exhilaration from the run, put her phone on speaker and called Special Agent Ortiz.

"Hi Jill, it's been about two weeks. Have you gotten into trouble already?"

"Haha. No I have a strange twist in the New Orleans case, and I wanted to make sure that I covered all the bases," Jill said providing the day's update.

"If there was anyone else but you on the other end of this phone call, I'd wonder what hallucinogen you were taking. Since I was your second call, then one, you have a game plan in your head and two, the New Orleans Police Department detectives were unable to satisfy the goals of your plan. So what do you want done?"

"I want someone to give me access to the security cameras at the International Airport. If I can find the man in the video, then the FBI will know that a man on Interpol's and your list is likely in the area. I'm speaking of your most wanted list. Then I want you to set up a sting operation to catch this guy and completely destroy the Midwest drug distribution and arrest or kill everyone involved in drug smuggling."

"Is that all?" asked Ortiz sarcastically.

"Yes, that's all I want," Jill said with cheer in her voice.

Jill heard this big sigh and then a dial tone. Special Agent Ortiz had hung up on her. What did that mean? Was she carrying on with Jill's requests? She stood there looking at her phone and realized how stupid that was. So she stood up and stretched and headed inside for a shower. She'd give the agent an hour before she went to the trouble to think of a new game plan.

She was in her kitchen ninety minutes later preparing her lunch, when her phone rang. Great she thought looking at the green avocado fruit all over her hands from cutting one up. She licked one finger and then reached over to answer the phone.

"This is Jill Quint," she called out while searching for a paper towel to get her hands clean.

"You're lucky I have a big enough reputation in the FBI to survive a weird request like this one and one that is out of my territory. If you'll take your laptop with the identity software into Sheriff Arstand's office, he'll connect to the Sheriff in New Orleans in charge of airport security so that you can scan their cameras. They have thirty days in storage so see if you can find your man. If you can, we may take more steps, but find your man first."

"On my way," and Jill was out the door within ten minutes and on her way to the Sheriff's office.

Thirty minutes later she was connected to airport security video storage unit and was flying through their archive. She got multiple hits for their suspect and it was so obvious, Jill was amazed, he'd never triggered some kind of alert. He was seen on the cameras every Tuesday and Thursday. He appeared to arrive on Tuesday and depart on Thursday based on the direction he was walking. Did that mean that a shipment arrived every Tuesday or Wednesday?

Today was Thursday which meant that if she watched long enough she would see him pass through, but to Jill that wasn't important. A shipment would be arriving on the coming Tuesday or Wednesday night. If the DEA or police could have a team in place, then they would likely catch the men involved.

She called Special Agent Ortiz and said, "Mr. Ricardo Rodriguez moves in and out of the New Orleans airport every Tuesday and Thursday. That suggests to me that the shipment is arriving at the plantation dock on Tuesday or Wednesday of next week. Is that enough time for someone to have a team in place?"

"I can't discuss the details of an op with a civilian, but I'll just say that we're on it."

"Did you hear that sound?" Jill asked.

"What sound?"

"The sound of my eyes rolling, but if that's the way you want to play it go ahead. Give me a call next week and tell me you've captured the suspect and the world's a little bit safer."

"Will do," and they ended their call.

# CHAPTER 35

Jill was relaying her conversation later that day to Nathan. He shook his head at what a busy day she'd had and the potential of her work to end a large criminal enterprise. She made him proud to know her in so many ways. Then she had gone from the world of criminals to her plan for her wine expansion without a break. Wow, he felt lucky to know her, love her, and share the passion of wine with her.

He discussed her concepts against trends he was seeing in the wine market from other vintners and thought she was choosing the right grapes.

"The Viognier grape is notoriously hard to grow, so you may end up buying more juice there if you don't get the production out of your own vines. When are you going to begin experimenting with these new grapes?"

"I ordered the juice already so really as soon as it arrives. Are you planning on being my guinea pig?"

"You bet. Just have me taste once you think you have the right mix, some of those grapes you're mixing can be very acidic if you don't get it right. Spare me that stage," he said with a grin.

"Of course, do you think I'd poison you?" Jill leaned in and gave him an elbow and then her cell phone rang.

She frowned, looking at the clock, "I wonder who's calling so late. It's almost ten pm."

"This is Dr. Quint," Jill said thinking it might be a potential client.

"Hi Jill, it's Special Agent Ortiz and I have an update for you that I think you'll enjoy."

"Nathan is here with me, so I'm going to put you on speaker phone."

"So here's a summary of the night in Louisiana. Mr. Rodriguez and ten of his men are in Federal detention and the DEA is in possession of ten tons of various illicit street drugs with a value of about $200 million dollars. The DEA asked me to pass their thanks on to you for your help."

Jill paused for a moment thinking about the cache of drugs and said, "Today's Thursday, it wasn't supposed to be a shipment day. What happened?"

"Since you alerted law enforcement to expect Mr. Rodriguez at the airport today there were agents ready to tail him through the airport and get on his plane. He passed a newsstand and did a double take. So our guys moved closer to see what was concerning him. There's a front page, large headline story of the senator's unfortunate death in a fiery car accident."

"Wow, they published that news quickly."

"Yes, so he left the newsstand and made several phone calls, all in Spanish and we could neither hear no understand his words. Thirty minutes later he left the airport in a car rental shuttle bus and picked up a rental car and began heading north we thought to the plantation. We managed to get several undercover agents on the senator's property with about ninety minutes notice. Kudos to my brothers and sisters in the FBI, DEA, and State police that got the operation going with so little notice.

"He arrived on the dark property followed by two vans and

then they all sat and waited. Just after midnight, a ship pulled into the dock and began unloading pallets of fertilizer."

"Except they weren't."

"Except it was a pallet of cocaine, methamphetamine, and fentanyl all headed north for distribution."

Jill clapped her hands in glee hearing about the arrests and seizure of the drugs and paused to ask, "Were any agents injured?"

"A few were bitten to death by mosquitoes and other bugs, but no alligators got any of the men nor did Rodriguez and his men. They weren't armed and didn't have night vision equipment to outrun the law."

"That's all great news! The case is finally closed. A man gets poisoned by nutmeg and that paves the way for the destruction of a drug distribution ring that's earned over a billion dollars for the Mexican drug lords over its existence. In the end, the senator finally did something right that permitted the end to this ring."

"Kudos to the men and women in Louisiana and I've been asked to introduce you to some leaders in on the sting. They 'want you to have more than me in your Rolodex for when you spot a bad criminal that needs arresting.' That's a direct quote from the DEA."

Jill laughed and replied, "I'm just a simple winegrower. As long as I have you Special Agent Ortiz in my Rolodex, I don't seem to need anyone else. You take me at my word and get things in motion."

"Glad I could help my colleagues and I think that man who owns the special software is about to see new interest from the United States."

"I'll pass that on to Henrik! Do you know if Mrs. Cheval was notified about these circumstances related to the death of her son?"

"I'll check back with my colleagues and suggest that they do that. It might ease her heart a little to know that his death was the tip of the iceberg that allowed the authorities to uncover a large drug ring. It won't bring back her son, but perhaps it will bring her some solace."

They said a few more words and then ended the call.

Jill had been typing slowly while she was on the phone with Ortiz. She paused a moment reading what she wrote and then hit one more key.

"I just dropped a note to Jo, Angela, Marie, and Alicia letting them know what happened. They each had a role in ending this drug distribution ring."

Nathan picked up his wine glass and gestured that she do the same. Once she raised it, he said "To you Dr. Jill Quint. Thank you for making our world just a little better today and every day." The toast led to a kiss, followed by an adjournment to his bedroom.

The End

ALSO BY ALEC PECHE

**<u>Jill Quint, MD Forensic Pathologist Series</u>**

Time's Up (prequel short story)

Vials

Chocolate Diamonds

A Breck Death

Death On A Green

A Taxing Death

Murder At The Podium

Castle Killing

Crescent City Murder

Sicilian Murder

Opus Murder

Forensic Murder

Return to the Scene of the Crime (short story)

Embers of Murder

Ashes to Murder

Mint Death

**<u>Damian Green Series</u>**

Red Rock Island

Willow Glen Heist

The Girl From Diana Park

Evergreen Valley Murder

Long Delayed Justice

**<u>Michelle Watson Series</u>**

Now You Don't See Me

Where Did She Go?

How Did She Get There?

**<u>Dog Humor</u>**

Eat, Play, Poop: Letters to my parents from camp

**<u>New Urban Fantasy Series - Stephanie Jones</u>**

The Awakening at Lake Tahoe (short story)

Witch's Medicine (2024)

# ABOUT THE AUTHOR

I reside in Northern California with my rescue dog and cat. I love to travel, play sports, read, and drink wine and beer. I enjoy the diversity of the world and I'm always watching people and events for story ideas. All of my stories are generated by my imagination, I don't use AI to write books.

If you would like to sign up for my bi-weekly blog and announcement of new books, please follow this link: https://www.AlecPecheBooks.com

While you're waiting for the next story, if you would be so kind as to leave a review for this book, that would be great. I appreciate all the feedback and support. Reviews buoy my spirits and stoke the fires of creativity.

Readers that sign up for my blog receive a free prequel novelette for the Jill Quint Series.

Amazon Author Profile

Author Profile on Goodreads

Author Profile on BookBub